—— The ——
Downfall of a Hustler

G Money

Fulton Books, Inc.
Meadville, PA

Published by Fulton Books 2020

ISBN 978-1-64654-458-5 (paperback)
ISBN 978-1-64654-459-2 (digital)

Printed in the United States of America

CHAPTER 1

Word spread throughout West Savannah that Rich was being released from federal prison. Everybody was anticipating the release of Rich kid. Rich was a legend in Savannah, Georgia, straight outta Fellwood Homes, and for many years, Rich and his crew ran the projects. Rich was like the mayor of his neighborhood; he put every nigga on "who wanted to get real" paper. The end of '96, all that came to an end when Rich was locked up and sentenced to ten years in federal prison. The ten years was finally over, and everybody knew that the hood was about to rise again. It was a regular day in the projects, and the basketball court was crowded as usual. A black Bentley pulled into the projects followed by a fleet of luxury vehicles. The way the cars maneuvered through the rough streets of Fellwood Homes, you would have thought the president was in town. The cars came to a complete stop, and everybody was looking and waiting to see who would step out the cars. The car door finally opened, and Rich stepped out of the car, along with his two beautiful daughters, Victoria and Paris, and auntie Donna. Everybody outside started chanting his name, "Richard, Richard, Richard, Richard." Rich took a deep breath and thought to himself, *Damn, it feels good to be home.* Rich looked around; so much has changed over the course of ten years.

Everybody welcomed him with open arms. Rich gave everybody daps and hugs as he made his way through the crowd of people. His daughters have blossomed into beautiful young women, and his auntie Donna looked as she hasn't aged since he was gone looking young as ever. Donna was Rich's mother baby sister. She took care of

Rich after his mother passed away. They have a special bond. Every bailer, drug dealer, and handyman in the projects wanted to make Donna his woman, but she wasn't having it. She was saving herself for a special man to be a part of her life. Later that night, everybody showed up to the party at the ballroom of the Savannah Civic Center. Rich took the mic from the DJ and asked to have everyone's attention. The room got quiet as everybody hung on his every word.

"I want to thank everyone for coming out tonight to celebrate this special moment with me. I really appreciate it from the bottom of my heart. While I sat behind those walls, all your prayers and thoughts really helped me get through those hard times and when I was at my lowest moments. I want to tell all of you thank you."

The music started blasting through the speakers. Everybody started to get their groove on with that same ole two-step. Rich really enjoyed himself; he was with the people he love the most—his two daughters, Victoria and Paris, who are now twenty and eighteen.

Rich said, "Victoria and Paris."

"Yes, Daddy."

"I missed you two so much."

"Daddy, we missed you so much also."

"Victoria, how's college?"

"It's great, Dad. I love going to Georgia Southern University. It has been a wonderful experience."

"Enjoy this college time because once it's gone, you can't get it back. And, Paris, my soon-to-be high school graduate, how is school going?"

"Dad, it's awesome. Now that you are home, you can come with me to check out some of the colleges."

"What do you want to do when you finish college?"

Paris said, "Daddy, I want to be a teacher," and Victoria replied, "I want to be a lawyer."

"Great choices. Paris, you can help Daddy with his publishing company, and, Victoria, you can help Daddy with his legal representation."

Paris asked "Daddy, do you have a publishing company?"

"No, not yet, but I will have one soon. Paris, you haven't changed not one bit with all your questions."

"Really, Daddy?" They both smiled at each other and embraced each other with big hugs. "Dad, I just be wanting to know things."

"Okay, baby girl."

You can tell from all the love Rich was getting that he was truly missed. All the major players who was getting real paper came to the party with gifts and money. Every bad bitch in the city wanted to fuck Rich, even the ones who were married. Rich was really bossed up that night. He had his right-hand man, Dollar, with him. Dollar came home two years before Rich. Dollar was the one who put the party together for his man Rich. Dollar is what you call a stand-up guy. I'm talking about sharp to a tee; Dollar had Rich back to the end no matter the situation. His man Kareem came home eight months prior. Kareem was what you call true to the game. He stood by everything he has said or ever did. Kareem had moved to Atlanta with Keke after he was released from federal prison. Kareem was solid as they came. Police ass Smitty's whereabouts were unknown. When it came to Smitty, Rich always said to himself he'll "kill him if somebody ain't did it before him police ass nigga." Smitty got sentenced to twenty-five years. But after cooperating with law enforcement, he got his time cut to thirteen years. Alexis moved to Dallas to start a new life, but her day was coming sooner than she thought. She thought she got away with that snitching shit. Her ass was fish-greased as soon as she popped her head up from underground. Rich's bodyguard, Big Al, was watching his back to perfection. Rich met Big Al in federal prison. He used to look after Rich's man, Arkee, who got a life sentence. Arkee introduced the two.

Arkee told Rich, "This is one solid dude. You need him on your team once you get back on the outside."

The two exchanged information, and Rich told Big Al once he got out, he'd look him up, and that's just what he did. Rich faded off into his uncle Blade's house with big Al leading the way. Five of Rich's li'l homies were in the house waiting on him. They each owed him $25,000. When he walked in, they greeted him and they each tossed bags in his direction.

"Damn, I see you niggas been getting to the money since I been gone. I like that."

Rich groomed his li'l homie to perfection. They stayed down to themselves and got money. They didn't let anybody stand in their way. Rich tossed the bags to Big Al, who went to put the money up. He chopped it up with his li'l homies for a minute and then was right back out the door to do him. As the day winded down, Rich made his rounds. When he got ready to leave, he saw a lot of people standing around this fly kid with a pretty slim thick chick on his side. The chick happened to be his best friend, Tracy. Tracy was always on his side pretending to be his girlfriend. Rich called Dollar over.

"Yo, Dollar, who's the dude over there with the red polo jogging suit on?"

"Li'l Sevyn. He runs a weed spot in the east side. He owns a few barbershops and hair salons. He's a cool li'l fella. He was an inspiring book writer, but he lost interest and stopped writing."

"Maybe one day I can get him back on the right track because it's major money to be made in the book publishing business. One day, maybe he can tell my story."

"Yeah, Rich, that would be dope. His barbershop and hair salon is having a cookout next week."

"Okay! Me and the guys will fall through."

"Yeah, do that. And who is the girl he got with him."

"I don't know but I like what I see."

"Man, Dollar, you crazy."

CHAPTER 2

It was a nice sunny day outside, so Sevyn decided to hit up the car wash and then head to the hair salon. Meanwhile, back at the hair salon, Tracy and Rebecca are preparing for today so they would be ready when their clients came through.

"Hey, Becky, have you seen Sevyn lately?"

"No."

"Me neither. It's been about three weeks since I last seen him. Speaking of the devil."

"You mean God." She laughed. "Bitch, bye."

"Girl, I gotta crush on Sevyn's sexy ass. There goes his ass pulling up in the parking lot."

Sevyn got out the car and started walking across the parking lot, turning heads. Becky stood up and just watched. Goddamn Sevyn know he was fine as hell. When Sevyn walked into the hair salon, both women spoke at the same time.

"Hey, Sevyn."

"Wazzup wit it, ladies? How are y'all doing? We doin' better now that you are here." Rebecca wanted to say so bad, *I'll be doing a whole lot better if I could get that dick up outcha*, but she kept her thoughts to herself.

"Y'all missed a nigga?"

"Boy, please, not at all."

"Tracy, speak for yourself," Rebecca said. "Hell yeah, I missed you."

Sevyn smiled turned around and walked into his office and sat behind his desk. Rebecca had a thing for Sevyn. Rebecca was a stallion with her big ass, big tits, cute face, and slim waist. She turned heads and stopped traffic everywhere she went. Rebecca had a man, but they were separated. When it came to Sevyn, she didn't give a damn about her man. The reality is, Tracy missed Sevyn and Sevyn knew it.

"Girl, all Sevyn got to do is give me a chance, and I'll put this pussy on him and have him calling for the lord."

"Bitch, you is crazy. Rebecca, is you coming to the cookout next week. If so, who are you inviting?" Tracy changed the subject. She got tired of Rebecca talking about Sevyn.

She was jealous because she liked Sevyn, but Sevyn only looked at her as a best friend, nothing more, nothing less.

"I'm inviting my best friend, Tara. She has an 11:00 a.m. appointment. You'll get a chance to meet her."

While the ladies were talking, Sevyn shot by. But before he could walk out the door, Tracy asked, "Are you coming back?"

"Yeah, later on," he replied.

Time had flown by, and before you knew it, it was Saturday and smoke filled the air from the barbecue. Rebecca saw her best friend had pulled up and parked, so she went to meet her. When the two approached each other, they greeted and embraced each other and then headed back over to Tracy.

"Hey, Tracy, this is my best friend Tara and, Tara, this is my friend and coworker Tracy."

"Nice to meet you, Tracy."

"Nice to meet you also, Tara," replied.

Tara talked the entire time Rebecca was doing her hair. Tracy just listened as Tara bragged about the car she drove and how much money she had and how she didn't take a shit from no nigga. Tracy made a mental note to stay from around this bitch. *She just moved back to Savannah and is already getting on my nerves.*

Later that evening, the shop was empty. Sevyn walked in and started talking to Tracy. "Yo, Lady T, wazzup?"

"Nothing much, Sevyn. Long time no see."

"I know, right? I have been so busy. So, Tracy, how's the new job coming along?"

"It's goin' great. Thanks for putting me on."

Sevyn looked up and said, "Anytime, Lady T. You know I got you."

"I know. Hey, Sevyn, my family is having a cookout next week. Maybe you can roll with me if you're not busy."

Sevyn replied, "Sounds like a plan, best friend."

One week later

"Yo, Tracy, this cookout is jumping."

"I know, right?"

Just as Sevyn was about to say something, he spotted the prettiest girl God had ever made. "Aye, Tracy, hold that thought for one second."

"Here you go again, always chasing a pretty face and fat azz."

Sevyn turned around with the biggest smile on his face and yelled out, "Hater!"

As Sevyn approached the young lady, first thing he noticed was her hazel eyes and pretty smile. Everything about her said wifey. Sevyn thought to himself, if he played his cards right, this could be his potential wife. Sevyn stood six feet and three inches with the frame of a pro athlete and the swag of a dope boy. As Sevyn was about to open his mouth, a black Lexus LS 430 pulled up.

"Ms. Jones, here is your car." She hopped in and pulled off with looking back as if Sevyn was never standing there. Sevyn returned to the tent where he left Tracy standing. He saw she had the biggest smile on her face. The smile on her face was saying, *That's what your ass gets, mister.*

"I can get any girl I want." He laughed. "Tracy, you just mad you couldn't pull me," he said as they joked around. "Tracy, wazzup? Do you know shawty that hopped in that Lexus?"

"Yeah, I know her. That's Tara. Rebecca's friend from out of town."

"Oh, okay. Damn, she sexy."

Tracy sucked her teeth.

"Why you suckin' your teeth?"

"Nothing, Sevyn! Nothing."

"Aye, fresh oh lord, what is it now, Tracy?" Sevyn knew a shit-load of questions was about to be asked once Tracy called him by his nickname she gave him. And she felt the same way when he called her Lady T. Sevyn is the only person who called her that.

"On a serious note, Sevyn, when is you going to give the game up?"

"Tracy, we have had this same conversation so many times."

"I know and you keep giving me the same answer."

"Soon. Tracy, I'm making a change. It's just taken me sometime. Change don't happen overnight, baity girl. It takes time."

"I know but I want you to be safe out here because these streets are dangerous."

"Well, you want to know what I think?"

"What, Tracy?"

"All right, don't be such a smartass black ass nigga."

"I'm not black, I'm brown-skinned."

"I don't know who the hell lied to you, but whoever it was must be talkin' 'bout the palm of your hand." She laughed.

"Whatever you like it."

"Sevyn, please. You think you all that."

"Nope, I know I'm all that."

Tracy blushed listening to the comment come out of Sevyn's mouth. But she knew he was telling the truth.

"I think you need to start back writing books. I think you will make a great author one day."

"Me too. Maybe I'll give it some thought. Writing books takes times and dedication, something I don't have right now. When I'm ready, I'll get back to it."

"Sevyn, you gatcha pistol with you?" The question caught Sevyn totally off guard.

"Yeah, why?"

"Because ever since you returned to the tent, those three guys leaning on that smoke gray Tahoe have been watching you and pointing over here."

"Trust me, Tracy, them niggas don't want these problems because I really hate to fuck up this cookout. Tracy, what are they doing now? They leaning up off the truck one by one."

Sevyn reached under his shirt, clutching his 45-caliber pistol. They started heading Sevyn's way. "Tracy, if they come any closer, Imma start squeezing out this bitch."

As they approached the tent and got within feet of Tracy, Sevyn slid the safety off his pistol and pulled it out slow. The three dudes stopped in midstep and held up their hands. The slim Kat with the Tom Ford frames on spoke with the smoothest tone ever.

"Hold up, playboy. We come in peace. We just have a message for you. A message from my nigga Rich. He want you to holla at him."

"Who is Rich? And why does he want me to come holla at him?"

"I guess he'll let you know when y'all meet up. Rich does understand that time is money, and he doesn't want to waste your time. Here's $5,000 for your time. Here take this card. The address is on it."

"Wait, 456 Fellwood Homes? That's the projects."

"Yeah, I know."

"With all due respect, tell yo man Rich I'm not coming over there."

Why not? It's just the projects. I mean, you gotta pistol, right?"

"Yeah."

"Fall through and stop being so scary tough guy." He laughed. "We out."

When the three men were out of sight, Sevyn just stood there, ashamed, knowing he just let Tracy see his true colors. Tracy burst out laughing.

"You scary li'l punk. Why you so scared to go to the projects? My fourteen-year-old son goes over to Fellwood Homes by his self all the time."

Sevyn turned around and said, "Shut the hell up. Have you ever gone to Fellwood Homes project?"

"Yeah, boy, plenty of times. Sevyn, are you goin' to the projects or what?"

"Yeah, I have no choice. I took the money, right?"

"Okay, good, because I'm ready to go shopping."

"Excuse me?"

Tracy totally ignored Sevyn and kept talking. "I need new shoes, a bag, and that new iPhone."

"Oh, really?"

"Hell yeah, really."

"I like how you make plans with my money."

"We a team, right?"

"I guess, Tracy."

"Okay then, put me in the game, Coach," she said.

The next day, Sevyn stepped out the house so fresh and so clean. Gucci from head to toe. He approached his S550 Benz. He spotted the young lady from the cookout riding by. He screamed, "Shawtyyy!" at the top of his lungs. She stopped and backed up. As she got near Sevyn, she brought her car to a complete stop, and the window rolled down.

"Is that how you get a woman's attention?"

"No, not at all, but I had to scream so you wouldn't get away from me. How are you doing? My name is Sevyn, but my best friend calls me Fresh."

"Fresh!"

"Yeah, Fresh."

"Why Fresh?"

"Because whenever she sees me, I'm always dressed in nothing but the best."

"Your best friend is a female?"

"Yeah, her name is Tracy, but I call her Lady T."

"Aww, how nice. You sure you're not fucking your best friend? I know how those best friend situation be."

"No, trust me, she is just my best friend."

"Okay, I hear ya, Mr. Fresh."

"I see somebody got jokes."

"I do."

"I like that."

"Oh, you do?"

"Sure do. I like Sevyn better."

"That what I'll call you. My name is Tara."

"Tara!"

"That's right, the one and only."

"That's such a cute name."

"Whatever! Don't try and butter me up."

"I'm tryna give you a compliment. I like the name Tara."

"So, Fresh, I mean Sevyn," she laughed, "is that your Benz?"

"Yes, ma'am. So, Ms. Hazel Eyes, I mean Tara, is that your Lexus?"

"I'm driving it, ain't I?"

"That don't mean nothing. People ride around showing off stunnin' in other people car every day, sweetie."

"Well, this is my car, and I'm not your sweetie."

"You will be in due time."

"Yeah, whatever!"

"Tara, what are you doing later, if you don't mind me asking?"

"Nothing much. I have no plans."

"Okay. So is it cool if I get your number and hit ya later?"

"That's cool."

"Maybe we can go out and get a bite to eat and have a drink or two."

"Are you asking me out on a date?"

"Yes, I am, Hazel Eyes."

"Then a date it is."

"How about 8:00 p.m.?"

"Sounds good to me. Hey, Sevyn, don't have me waiting on you all night."

"Trust me, I won't, Hazel Eyes."

Tara couldn't help but start blushing, loving the new nickname Sevyn had given her. "All right, Sevyn, I'll see you later." Tara pulled off slow, and Sevyn just stood there smiling, thinking to himself, *Damn, I'm the man.*

Moments later, Sevyn jumped into his car and sped off, jamming to his favorite song by Master P, "Gangstas Need Love Too." Sevyn had the prettiest Benz ever—peanut butter inside, twenty-two-inch Asanti rims with a candy wine berry burgundy to top it off. Sevyn had that candy looking good enough to eat. Sevyn started bobbin' his head to the music. He switched lanes, making a left on to 37th Street to hit the highway. Sevyn was swerving in and out of traffic, feeling the music. When he got on to the highway, he made a quick stop to the store to get gas, play his lottery, cash 4 numbers, and purchase three lottery scratch-off tickets. When he got to the counter, he told the cashier to give him $25 on pump four and told the cashier he wanted to play cash 4.

She said, "Sir, what are the numbers to play?"

"Let me get 1717, 1010, $1 straight and $1 straight box and three jumbo bucks, that's it."

"Okay, your total is $34. Here you go, sir. Thank you, come again."

Sevyn approached the gas pump and began pumping his gas. When he was finished, he jumped back on the highway, thinking to himself, *Today is my day. Imma hit the lottery today.* When Sevyn made it close to Tracy's neighborhood, he flipped open his cellphone and dialed Tracy's number. After the third ring, Tracy answered the phone, singing and reciting the words to Trina's song, "Da Baddest Bitch."

Sevyn burst out laughing and said, "You wish."

"You know what, Sevyn, fuck you."

"Baby girl, I know you wish you could. But anyway, I'm on the way to pick you up, so we can go check the dude Rich out. I'll be there in twenty minutes."

"Okay, fo sho. I'm 'bout to get dressed now."

"Twenty minutes later, Sevyn pulled and hit the horn. Tracy's front door flew open.

"Sevyn, she coming," Tracy's fourteen-year-old son, Ny'quan, shouted. Seconds later, Tracy came out the house, and Sevyn's mouth dropped. Sevyn thought to himself, *Damn, Tracy's sexy as hell.* He never really looked at Tracy like that, but for some reason, her pretty round ass is sitting right in her Christian Dior jeans, and he was noticing it. She jumped in and closed the door.

"So wazzup, Fresh? How you feeling?"

"I'm feeling like I look. Good girl, what you expect?" he laughed.

"I guess. Hey, Sevyn, let's go get something to eat. Where you want to go?"

"Red Lobster."

"You got Red Lobster money?"

"Nope, but you do."

Fifteen minutes later, the two pulled up to Red Lobster and went inside. The waiter asked how many seats, and Tracy said two. The waiter said, "Okay, right this way." When they were seated, the waiter said, "Someone will be with you shortly to take your order." While they waited on the waiter to come take their order, Sevyn began to ask Tracy about the shawty from the cookout.

"Aye, Tracy."

"Wazzup, Sevyn?"

"You remember the shawty from the cookout with the hazel eyes?"

"Yeah, the one who left you standing on the curb."

"You know what, Tracy, go to hell."

"Whatever! But anyway, what about her?"

"I caught her riding up my street and hollered at her."

"Yeah, right."

"For real, we going on a date tonight at 8:00 p.m."

"Be careful. It's something about that girl that just don't sit right with me."

"What makes you feel that way? You don't even know her."

"You right, I don't know her, but I've been in her presence a few times and I get fucked-up vibes when I'm around her. Even filing about her says gold digger money-hungry bitch."

Sevyn thought, *Maybe Tracy is jealous.* And just before Sevyn opened his mouth, Tracy spoke. "And I'm not jealous," as if she was reading Sevyn's mind. "Sevyn, have I ever told you anything wrong?"

"No!"

"Okay! You then. You can just thank me later."

After talking for some time over a nice meal, they wrapped things up at Red Lobster and headed out. They made an exit out of Red Lobster's park, heading up White Bluff Road. They noticed an accident ahead and had to make a detour. As they approached exit 5, they made a sharp right onto Bay Street, the main street that leads to the projects. Sevyn's eyes got big. They saw drug dealers and crackheads everywhere.

"Tracy, do you see apartment 456?"

"Hold up, slow down, 452, 454, 456—there it is to the right."

They parked and jumped out, and Sevyn and Tracy saw li'l kids playing in dirt with no shoes on. One kid even ran up to Sevyn and asked for a dollar.

"Here you go, li'l man."

"Thank you."

Sevyn knocked on the door four times and then took a step back. A voice from behind the door said, "Who is it?"

"It's me Sevyn. Rich is expecting me. Is he here?"

"Hold up." After two minutes of waiting, the door finally opened. "Come in," the short stocky man said. "Have a seat. He'll b-b-b-b-be right with you shortly." The man stuttered so bad Sevyn and Tracy wanted to burst out laughing, but they heard someone come in through the back door. When they turned around, they saw a tall, slim-built black kat, about six feet and four inches, walk in Tom Ford from head to toe with waves in his head that will make a bitch seasick. He had a mouth full of gold teeth, a Rolex watch, and a gold chain. Everything about him said drug dealer.

"Yo, wazzup, Sevyn? I see you brought a guest with you."

"Yeah, this is my best friend Tracy."

"Fo sho. Wazzup, Tracy? I'm Rich, nice to meet you both. I see y'all met my cousin Stutter Box. Wazzup, Stutter Box?"

"Wazzup, R-R-R-R-Rich. What's g-g-g-good?"

"Man, you gon' have to learn sign language with all that stuttering."

"F-F-F-F-Fuck you, Rich."

"Say, Sevyn, I sent my li'l homies to come holla at ya because I have a job for you."

"What kind of job? And how much does it pay?"

"The job pays $25,000. But being that I paid you $5,000 up front, I only owe you $20,000."

"So what's the job?"

"I heard you are pretty good at writing books and telling stories."

"Fo sho. I'm one of the best to ever do it."

"So I need you to tell my story, that's it."

"That's it?"

"Yeah, that's it. I'm starting a publishing company and I really want you to be a part of it. I'm publishing books for the up and coming authors. I think this would be a good opportunity for you and me. So what do you say?"

"I'm all in, let's do it."

"I just came home from doing a federal prison bid, and I'm trying to get my life back on the right track. So I'll take you back to the beginning where it all started at. I remember it like it was yesterday."

CHAPTER 3

It was the fall of '95. October eighth, to be exact.

"Daddy, can you buy us a bike?"

"You know Daddy got y'all."

"We want a big bike, not li'l cheap bike like last time."

"You know what, Rich, them girls got you wrapped around their fingers."

"Anything for my baby girls."

While Rich was in the room bagging up cocaine, his phone started ringing. "Auntie Donna, bring me my phone." Rich flipped open his phone and said hello.

"Hey, Rich, this Tina."

"Wazzup, cousin?"

"Kareem want you."

"Hold on, wait a minute."

But before Rich could ask Tina, he was cut short The guy started talking. "What's good, my guy?"

"Chillin'. What's good?"

"Nothing much. Man, Rich, I need to see ya. You know a nigga just came home." *Click.*

Rich waited for a few minutes and then called Tina back. "Yo, Tina, who was I talking to?"

"That was Kareem."

"You talkin' bout Kareem from Fellwood Homes?"

"Yeah, that's my nigga."

"Run back outside and go get him."

Seconds later, Kareem jumped back on the phone. "Yo, Rich kid, wazzup, baby?"

"Just coolin' my nigga. My bad, Reem. I ain't know that was you."

"Man, I'm home. When you got out?"

"Yesterday."

"I'm home is West Savannah. My house right next to the store on Fell Street. Me, my two daughters, and my auntie Donna."

"You got Donna with ya?"

"Yeah, tell Donna I'm on the way to see her."

"Okay. Donna" Kareem home. What Kareem? Kareem form Fellwood. He on the way to here to see you. That's my nigga. I can't wait to see him. Twenty minutes later a blue Honda pulled up. Kareem hopped out along with Smitty. Rich never really trusted Smitty but he was cool with Kareem so Rich thought to himself what the hell. Rich, Kareem, Smitty, and Donna talked for hours before Kareem and Smitty had to leave. Kareem shook Rich hand before they parted ways. Aye Rich Kid my baby out of town in the hospital sick. Ima go spend some time with her. Ok! Fasho give hr. my blessing. I hope she gets well soon. I will. I will hitchu up when I get back in town.

Rich's daughters, Victoria and Paris, both played soccer. Rich, Donna, and Rich's fiancée, Alexis, loved supporting the girls. Victoria was the older sister. She was nine years old, and Paris was seven years old. One Saturday, after the game, Rich decided to take the girls out for ice cream to celebrate their victory. Paris jumped in the car first, screaming, "We won! We won!" Vicky jumped in the car right after her.

"I don't know why you jumpin' up and down screaming we won when you didn't even get in the game."

Paris sat back in her seat, quiet because her feelings were hurt. Rich finally stopped and turned around and looked Victoria in the face.

"Vitoria."

"Yes, Daddy?"

"As long as you walking the earth, don't ever let me hear you belittle your little sister. Do you understand me?"

"Yes, sir."

"Now tell her you sorry."

"I'm sorry, Paris, for makin' fun of you."

Now, Vicky, gave her a hug, and they went to get some ice cream. When they sat down at the table, Paris asked, "Daddy, way her pretty car at?"

"In the shop."

"Daddy, you brought her that car."

"Paris, why do you ask so many questions?"

"I don't ask so many questions."

"Yes, you do. Hey, Vicky, when we finish, y'all want to go to Auntie Donna's house?"

"Yeah."

"Victoria, y'all championship game next week. Y'all going to win?"

"Yes, sir."

"Okay, Imma see."

The next day at Donna's house, Rich walked in.

"Hey, Auntie!"

"Wazzup, big head ass boy!"

"Nothin' much. Way my babies at?"

"In the front room watchin' TV. Vicky and Paris, y'all daddy here."

They both came running in the kitchen.

"Daddy! Daddy, way you been?"

"Home."

All of a sudden, Paris came outta left field and asked, "Daddy, are you broke?"

"No, baby, Daddy not broke. Why would you ask that?"

"Because my mama said you was broke, and her boyfriend got more money than you."

"Oh really!"

"Yep."

"You heard that, Auntie Donna?"

"Yeah, I heard that, Latrell. Better quit talking around that girl." She knew Paris repeats everything she hears. "Imma have a talk with her." Latrell was Rich's baby mama. Rich met Latrell at Club 3D. They were together for six years. When Rich got locked up for trafficking cocaine, she thought he was goin' to get some time. So she decided to leave him for another drug dealer named Rocky Montana. Rich was only gone for five months before he was acquitted of all charges and released. When Rich came home, he decided that it would be best if he didn't have anything to do with Latrell anymore.

Two days later, Rich pulled up in front of Latrell's house in his new white Range Rover. He got out and knocked on the door. Latrell answered the front door wearing just a robe.

"Wazzup, Rich?"

"Nothing much. Do you mind if I come in?"

"No, come in."

"Look, Latrell, we need to talk about you talking around Paris and telling her I'm broke. We can't have that. It's not cool. I don't talk about you, so I'll appreciate it if you don't talk about me."

"So that's it, Rich? That's all you came over here for?"

"Yeah." Rich stood to his feet to leave. But before he turned to leave, Latrell busted open her robe, exposing her smooth nude body. Latrell's body was to die for.

"You mean to tell me you don't want this sweet pussy?"

"Naw! I can't do nothing with you."

"I'm cool on you. I'm out li'l mama juices."

"The girls have a championship game Saturday, and they would love for you to be there if you can. Peace out."

CHAPTER 4

It was Saturday afternoon, and the game was about to start. Rich looked to his left and saw Latrell and her boyfriend, Rocky Montana, walking up. When they got near, Latrell spoke.

"Wazzup, Rich? Wazzup, Donna?"

Rocky Montana looked at Rich and spoke. "What's good, my nigga?"

"Slow motion in this end."

"Sometimes slow motion better than no motion." Rich looked at Rocky Montana and nodded his head right on and then focused back on the game. Donna turned to Rich and asked, "Is that her li'l dirty boyfriend who she said had more money than you?"

"Yep! That's him." They both burst out laughing.

The game started, and Victoria was having a hard time keeping up. The coach put Paris in the game. She was on fire. She played the entire game. There was five seconds left, and the game was tied, 6–6. Counting down the last five seconds and just before the clock hit one, Paris kicked the winning goal to seal the championship. When the game was over, the coach came over and told Paris she was the star of the team. Victoria was jealous, and Rich could see it all over her face. Even though Rich hated to admit it, it was good to see Paris rub it in Victoria's face for once.

After the game, Rich dropped his daughters and Auntie Donna off to the house and headed to Fellwood Homes projects. Rich posted up in Fellwood like he owned the projects. He was what you called a ghetto celebrity. He didn't have the most money in the hood, but he was well respected, and that alone made him stand out from the rest. Every bitch in the projects lusted over Rich. He was like a dog in heat, always tricking his dick even though he had a fiancée. His fiancée worked in a different state. Rich always thought, what she doesn't know won't hurt her. Rich knew if his fiancée caught him cheating, she would have fucked him and the bitch up on site. Rich kept everything in the dark when it came to other hoes.

Three days later, Rich got an unexpected call from his fiancée. "Baby, I'm at the airport. Come pick me up."

"Huh?"

"Come pick me up."

"You back already?"

"Yeah, the job contract was terminated early."

"Damn." Rich knew playtime was over; the boss lady was home, and Rich knew not to disrespect his fiancée. Alexis was hell when she was well. About Rich, Alexis would kick ass from Maine to Spain. Disrespect and playing games weren't an option. Alexis told Rich if she ever caught him cheating, she was goin' to leave him and make his life a living hell.

"Baby, it feels good to be back home. Did you miss me while I was gone?"

"What kind of question is that? You know I missed you."

While Sevyn and Tracy listened to Rich talk, they heard gunshots ringing out in the projects, and it caught their attention. "Hey, Rich, I think it's getting pretty late. It's about time to roll."

"Man, Sevyn, it's six o'clock in the afternoon."

"I know, Rich, but I heard the crime rate is pretty high on this side of town. All heads turned when they heard the back door open.

"Rich kid, wazzup, fam?"

"Wazzup, Dollar? What's good?"

"Nothing much, same ole shit."

Sevyn immediately recognized the man's face. It was the slim kat from the cookout.

"Yo, Sevyn, wazzup, fool? I see you made it."

"Yeah, I made it."

"See, the projects ain't that bad. And who might this young lady be you got with you?"

"This my best friend, Tracy."

"I can talk for myself. My name is Tracy."

"How you doin', Ms. Tracy? My name's Donte, but my friends call me Dollar."

"Nice to meet you, Dollar."

"Nice to meet you too, Tracy. Ms. Tracy, I wouldn't be disrespecting you if I asked to take you out sometime, would I? You know, we can get to know each other a li'l better."

"No, you wouldn't be disrespecting me, not at all. As a matter of fact, I think it would be great to go out with you sometime."

"Okay, cool. Here's my number, get at me."

Tracy took the number as she blushed the entire time. Sevyn and Tracy got up, shook all three men's hand, and said, "Rich, we out fo sho."

"When y'all coming back?"

"What's today?"

"Sunday."

"Yeah. We'll be back next week Sunday, same time."

The car was silent as Tracy and Sevyn made their way back to the other side of town. Tracy began to talk. "I'm not goin' to fuck him."

"Tracy, what are you talking about? You haven't said one word since we got back in the car. And—" Tracy could tell that Sevyn was kind of jealous, and she liked every minute of it.

"Drop me off to Moon River Sports Bar and Grill. I need a drink."

When they got to Moon River, Tracy hopped out. "Call me after you wrap up your li'l playdate." It was 7:30 p.m., so Sevyn decided to call Tara. Tara answered the phone on the second ring as if she was waiting on Sevyn to call.

"Hello?"

"Wazzup, Ms. Tara?"

"Nothing much, waiting on you."

"Is that right?"

"Yep. So what time you picking me up and where from?"

"At 8:00 p.m., like you said."

"I stay on the west end of Ranchwood Apartment building 27. Just call me when you get outside."

Sevyn pulled up fifteen minutes later. "I'm outside, sweetie."

Tara came to the door and hopped in the car. "Didn't I tell you I'm not your sweetie."

"Girl, stop frontin'. You know you like it when I call you sweetie."

"Whatever! So, Mr. Sevyn, where are we going?"

"Downtown to the jazz bar."

"So, Sevyn, you like jazz?"

"Yeah, I love jazz." *Damn, I just sat in Tara's face and told her a bold-faced lie. I don't know a damn thing about jazz music.* Sevyn was trying to impress the beautiful woman he was out on the town with. Two hours had passed. The party of two ate dinner, laughed, and sipped on cocktail until it was time for the bar to close. Sevyn stopped the waitress and asked for the check. Sevyn looked at the check and said, "Damn, $127, sweetie. We been drinking our ass off." Sevyn paid the bill and tipped the waiter, and then they both headed out. Sevyn and Tara cruised the city, listening to the oldies as they reminisce about the night they just had. As Sevyn got closer to Tara's place, she cut the music and focused all her attention on Sevyn.

"Sevyn, I really enjoyed my evening with you, I must admit."

"Well, I enjoyed my evening as well, Ms. Hazel Eyes." He laughed. "Maybe we can do this again sometime."

When Sevyn pulled into Ranchwood Apartment, he was shocked when Tara asked him if he wanted to come up to her apartment and keep her company. Sevyn thought, *First, a dinner date and now an invite into her house. Today must be my lucky day.*

"You have a beautiful home."

"Thank you. Have a seat and make yourself at home. I'm goin' to slip into something a little more comfortable."

Sevyn's eyes damn near burst out of his head when Tara returned. *Damn, this muthafucka sexy.* Her cherry-red silk robe complemented every curve on her body. Sevyn's manhood was at attention. I'm talking about dick harder than a roll of quarters. She sat on Sevyn's lap and whispered in his ear, "I hope you have self-control." Sevyn was clueless as to why she said that, but he sure in the hell was going to find out. She grabbed his hand and told him to come, and then she led him to her bedroom where she had the slow jams playing. She pushed Sevyn down on his back and climbed on top of him. She began to suck on his neck, earlobes, and chest. The goddess eased down and began to lick his stomach and undo his belt buckle.

"Wait a minute, let me get the condom out my pocket."

"No, I hate condoms."

Sevyn wanted the pussy so bad that he went against everything he stood for and raw-dogged her. Tara jumped up on that dick like a pro. She began riding him slow, driving his mind in every direction. As she bounced up and down, her pussy got so wet that Sevyn could see her juices on his dick every time he looked down. Sevyn felt his nut about to come, so he flipped her over and began to dig deep into her pussy. Tara loved every minute of it. She began to talk. "Baby, fuck me, fuck me harder." Sevyn did as he was told and began pounding on her a like jackhammer.

"Baby, I'm about to come," she yelled.

Sevyn yelled, "Me too." In a matter of seconds, they both climaxed together.

The next morning, they both woke up, showered, and got dressed. Tara walked Sevyn outside to his car.

"Aye, Sevyn."

"Wazzup, sweetie?"

"I had an amazing night. When will I see you again?"

"Hopefully tonight." She gave him a kiss, and they both parted ways. Tara jumped in her car and backed up slowly. Sevyn blew her a kiss as she pulled off. Sevyn got in his car and realized he had seventeen missed calls and eight unanswered texts from his best friend, Tracy, so he decided to return her calls. It rang five times before she answered.

"What!"

"What you mean what? Sevyn, I called and texted you all last night to make sure your ass made it in safe after your little playdate."

"I left my phone in the car. And besides, I was busy. I didn't stay home. I stayed at her place."

"Did you fuck her?"

"Excuse me!"

"You heard me. Did you fuck her?"

"No!" Sevyn lied.

"All right. Don't say I didn't warn you."

CHAPTER 5

Tracy, you wanna go to Tanger Outlet? My treat."

"I know good and goddamn well it's your treat because a bitch broke. I don't get paid until next week. So tell me all about your li'l playdate."

"It was cool. We went to the jazz bar downtown. We had dinner and a few cocktails."

"I heard the jazz bar was really nice."

"You should go check it out."

"Maybe I can get Dollar to take me next weekend if I'm off." Sevyn's facial expression changed. "Loosen up, Sevyn. It's just a date."

"I'm just sayin'."

"What is you sayin', Sevyn?"

"Don't get homeboy fucked up."

"Boy, bye."

When they made it to the outlet, Sevyn spotted Rebecca's car. "Damn, Tracy Rebecca must be out here."

"She is. I texted her and told her to meet us out here so we all can catch up. I hope she don't think I'm buying her something." Tracy heard a voice from afar.

"Tracyyy!"

"Wazzup up, bitch?"

"Wazzup, sexy ass Sevyn?"

"Shit just coolin'." Sevyn started walking behind Rebecca, admiring her nice plump ass in her tight-fitting white jeans. Sevyn shot back. "Rebecca, wazzup, with ya sexy ass?"

Rebecca just blushed, taking in the question Sevyn just asked her. Rebecca replied, "Shid ya already know wazzup. Me and yo baby, that's wazzup."

The three shopped until the outlet was closed. Rebecca asked Tracy, "What are y'all about to do?"

"We about to head over to Moon River Sports Bar and Grill and have a few drinks."

"Oooh, I wanna go."

"Come on, follow us over there." When they got there, the sports bar was jam-packed as usual. A drunk couple was falling all over the place, trying to do karaoke, so they decided to hit the bar.

"Sevyn," asked the ladies, "what are y'all drinking?"

They both replied at the same time, "Rum punch."

"Man, dat weak shit."

"Well, what you drinking?"

"Gray goose and cranberry juice. A man's drink."

After they downed the first drink, they hit the dance floor. The ladies asked Sevyn, "I hope you got some free dance moves up your sleeve."

Sevyn replied, "I know a li'l something something."

Rebecca and Tracy had Sevyn in a sandwich—Rebecca in the front and Tracy in the back. Rebecca had that big ole azz all over Sevyn. Sevyn was beginning to have an erection, and Rebecca knew it. Sevyn decided to stop dancing. They all went and sat down and had another round while laughing and joking around. Sevyn told the ladies, "I'm tired. I haven't had that much fun in a long time."

The ladies both said, "I think we should do this again sometime."

"That would be great," Tracy said. "Sounds like a plan to me."

Rebecca said, "I'm down. Just let me know, but in the meantime, Imma get up outta here."

Sevyn asked Tracy, "Are you ready to go?"

She yelled out, "Hell yeah, let's go." Tracy looked at Rebecca and threw up the juices. "Yo, Rebecca, we out. Drive safe.

Sevyn left Moon River. He made a left on Broughton Street and headed toward the east side to drop Tracy off. When he pulled up in front of Tracy's doorstep, they gave each other a hug. Sevyn told Tracy he enjoyed her company and that he'd see her tomorrow.

"Tracy said, "Fo sho. Aye, Sevyn."

"Wazzup, Tracy?"

"Thanks for taking me shopping."

"It's all good. Yo treat next time."

Tracy smiled and then jumped out the car. Sevyn watched Tracy's ass jiggle the entire time as she headed to her front door. Sevyn said in a low tone, "Damn, Tracy's sexy as hell." When Sevyn pulled off from Tracy's house, his phone started vibrating. It was a text message from Rebecca tellin' him to meet her at the shop and that "I'm not taking no for an answer." The next text message came through: "I gotta get something out the shop and I left my key home." Sevyn wanted to text her back and tell her he was gone in for tonight, but he was still out, so he said, "What the hell, I can do one favor for her." Sevyn pulled up to the hair salon and saw Rebecca standing outside, leaning up against her car. He parked and got out and unlocked the door. They both went inside. Rebecca walked to her station, and Sevyn walked into his office to check his e-mails.

Sevyn spent fifteen minutes checking his e-mails. He never really paid Rebecca any attention. When he looked up, his eyes stretched outta his head. He was shocked to see Rebecca standing in the middle of his doorway buckass naked. Rebecca walked over to Sevyn's desk, turned around, and bust that pretty pink pussy open, exposing nothing but her wetness.

"So, Sevyn…"

"What, Rebecca?"

"So you mean to tell you don't want this pretty pink pussy?"

Sevyn was at a loss for words. Sevyn's dick was stiffer than a steel baseball bat. Nigga from Savannah, Georgia, always had a sayin', "Thinking with the wrong head will get your ass in trouble every time," and boy was they right. Rebecca dropped to her knees and pulled Sevyn's dick out and went to work. She started out slow and then began to speed up. Sevyn gripped his chair like he was on a roller-coaster ride. Rebecca was eatin' the dick up like there was no tomorrow. Sevyn watched as her head went up and down, taking every inch of his dick into her mouth. Sevyn had his hands on the back of Rebecca's head. She removed his hands from the back of her head. Caught up in the feeling, he gently placed his hands back on her head again.

"Did I tell you to grab the back of my head?"

"No," he replied.

"So move your hand. I don't need your help. I got this. Lemme run this show." Rebecca started finger-fucking herself with her two middle fingers. As her fingers slipped in and out her wetness, she moaned louder by the minute. Rebecca's pussy was so wet you could've heard it smacking. Sevyn reached into his desk and grabbed a condom. Rebecca took the condom out of Sevyn's hand and put it in her mouth and rolled it on Sevyn's dick like a pro. Sevyn slid out the chair onto the floor, flat on his back. She stood over him and then dropped down. Rebecca began to bounce on that dick like she had springs in her knees.

After twenty minutes of bouncing on that dick, she turned around on the dick without taking it out of her pussy. Sevyn was so amazed. He couldn't believe that this was Rebecca acting up like this. Rebecca's tight pussy gripped Sevyn's dick every time she slung that big ole azz back. She was ready to climax, so she jumped off the dick and bent over on her knees. Sevyn slid behind her and slowly entered her wetness. She began to moan loud and yell out Sevyn's name.

"Goddamn, Sevyn baby, please say my name. Say my name, baby."

"Oooh, shit, Rebecca baby, this pussy wet and good."

"Say it again."

"This pussy good, baby."

"Sevyn, I'm about to cum. I'm about to cum." In the middle of them climaxing, Rebecca yelled out, "Damn, Sevyn, this dick is good."

When they were finished, Sevyn stood up and realized the condom popped. He said to himself in a low tone, "Ain't this about a bitch. I just nutted in Rebecca. Damn!" What was supposed to have been an in-and-out thing turned into a two-hour fuck session.

*****

It was Friday, and Tracy just got a text from Dollar saying he wanted to see her. She texted back and said, "That's fine. I'm home. I'll text you the address." Dollar arrived thirty minutes later. When he pulled up, he saw Tracy fussing on the phone.

When Dollar got out of his navy blue 750i BMW, he walked up to Tracy, and she hung her phone up just in the nick of time to give him a nice big hug. He asked, "Is everything okay?"

"Yeah, I'm cool. It's just my punk ass baby daddy tripping about getting my son shit."

"You know what, Tracy, fuck 'em."

"It's all good, I got it. Thanks, Dollar."

"No problem, anytime."

Tracy and Dollar talked for hours about everything—common goals, the future, their hobbies, and favorite food.

"Hey, Dollar."

"Wazzup, Tracy?"

"You are a really cool dude."

"You know, I try to be. Well, it's getting late, and I have to work at 8:30 a.m. I hope to see you tomorrow. Give me a hug."

The two hugged for a quick second and then let each other go. Dollar's hand went into his pocket and pulled out five one hundred dollar bills. "Here this is for your son."

"Thank you, Dollar."

"You welcome."

"I'm gone, Li'l Mama."

"Okay, drive safe."

*****

Two days later, Sevyn decided to head back over to the projects, but this time, he took the ride alone. He decided to leave Tracy behind just in case Dollar was there. As Sevyn pulled up to park, he saw Rich and Dollar standing outside in front of the project building, smoking the finest weed. Sevyn took out his whip.

"Yo, Rich, what's good?"

"Shid this weed we smoking on."

"Dollar, wazzup, playboy?"

"Nothing much, li'l homie. Just tryna make a dollar."

Rich gave Dollar some dap and said, "I know that right. Aye, that weed you and Dollar smoking on smell good as hell. What's that?"

"Li'l homie, this is that OG Kush. You smoke, Sevyn?"

"Hell yeah! Let me hit that shit."

Dollar asked Sevyn, "Yo playboy, where Tracy at?"

Sevyn lied and said, "Tracy was at work."

As Dollar leaned up off the window seal, he realized he burned a hole in his shirt from the ashes. "Damn, Rich, I done fucked my shirt up."

"Man, Dollar, all that money you getting, I know you ain't tripping off no hole in your shirt."

"Yeah, yo right. Yo, Rich Kid, I'm out. I'm about to head back to check on the li'l homies."

Soon as Dollar started to walk off, Sevyn put out the blunt and began to follow Rich into the house. Rich and Sevyn sat down at the round table, and Rich continued his story, picking up where he left off. Dollar made his way through the projects' cuts, walking fast as hell because he knew this was Officer Giles's shift. Dollar thought, *He hates to have a run-in with Spike.* Spike was Officer Giles's dirty-ass partner.

Soon as Dollar stepped in the street, Spike swung the corner. Dollar turned around and took off running full speed. Spike jumped out the car, chasing him. When Spike hit the corner running full speed, he tripped up and busted his ass. When he got up, he was screaming at the top of his lungs. "Imma get ya, ya black son of a bitch!"

Dollar made it back to the other side of the projects to holla at his playa partner, CJ. CJ was the youngest in Rich's crew. CJ asked Dollar, "What's wrong with him and why was he out of breath?"

"Man, CJ, I just had to haul ass from Spike. That bitch-ass nigga bust his ass."

"Damn! You faked his ass out like that?"

"Hell yeah!"

"How did ya do that?"

"You know how Monk raggedy car always leave oil all over the parking lot pavement?"

"Yeah!"

"Spike's bitch ass jumped off the curb and landed in the oil and slipped. When I got away, I fell to the ground laughing."

"Dollar, he gon' have it out for you."

"Man, fuck that cracka, CJ."

Rich and Sevyn sat down at the round table, and Rich continued his story, picking up where he left off.

CHAPTER 6

Three weeks later, Rich's phone was going off like crazy. When he flipped his phone open, the caller ID said "Unavailable Caller." Rich answered the phone, and before he could ask who it was, Kareem screamed through the phone.

"Wazzup, Rich kid?" You can tell from the tone of Kareem's voice he was smiling from ear to ear.

"You know. Wazzup, Kareem?"

"I'm gettin' money."

"I wish I could say the same thing."

"Aye, Rich kid, if I had yo hands, I'll cut my hands off."

"Man, Kareem, gone 'head with all that bullshit. You funny as hell."

"I ain't lying, Rich kid. I'll turn those bitches in." He laughed.

"Rich kid, da hoe still love you?"

"Come on, this Rich kid the hoes gon' always love me. Aye, Kareem, how's your daughter doing?"

"She is doing real good. She really came a long way. She come home from the hospital tomorrow."

"Kareem, that's great. Me and the girls are going to come by and visit her when she come home. In the meantime, what ya doin' tonight?"

"Whatever you doing. I'm fuckin with you."

"Okay, cool. Let's step out tonight. You know the strip club gon' be off the chain tonight. Master P is goin' to be live in concert tonight. The whole city knows Club 3D is the place to be on the weekend. Later that night, Rich met Kareem and Smitty up at the club in the VIP section of the parking lot so they could valet they cars. Rich, Kareem, and Smitty stepped in the club, shutting that bitch down. Rich stood out from Kareem, Smitty, and everybody in the club because of his jewelry. Rich had on a Cuban link worth $50,000 and a diamond-incrusted Rolex watch worth $40,000. Every bitch in the club wanted rich. And half of the niggas hated him for no reason. Everybody knew Rich was a fool with a pistol in his hand, and he dared anybody to try 'em. While in the club, Kareem whispered to Rich, "I see my man Sanchez from Miami I was in the feds with. He got stupid numbers. He got bricks for $18,000.

"Imma go holla at him."

"Yeah, most definitely do that."

Rich's favorite song came on in the dub by Master P, "Break 'Em Off." Rich threw his hands high in the air and yelled out, "That's my shit."

Kareem returned as soon as the song went off.

"So, Kareem, wazzup, fool? What Florida boy talking bout. He want me to come check him soon as he get back to Miami. 2 days later Sanchez told Kareem he had a 9:00am flight to catch back to Miami. So you would have to drive down to Miami and meet me. Sanchez texted Kareem the address and he jumped straight on the road as planned. He would've took a first class flight but he was on federal probation and it prohibited him from flying. When Kareem arrived to Miami he met Sanchez at a yacht that was docked at the port of Miami. Sanchez greeted. My friend I see you made. Hell yeah! That ride was long as hell. Look at the bigger picture you are about to become a very rich man my friend. Sanchez showed Kareem around the yacht as the talked about business. Damn Sanchez I ain't know you was doing it like this big. Sanchez had the baddest Cuban bitches walking around half naked. Maids cleaning and bartenders pouring endless drinks to keep the guest entertained. When the two finally sat down to discuss business Sanchez asked Kareem what can I do for you my friend. Wasting no time Kareem got straight to the point Well Sanchez you know I just came home 2 months ago and I'm starving dawg. I need a push. It's plenty money to be made in Savannah. Me and my Rich already got the setup ready to go down.

Ok this is what I'll do for you Kareem because I like you and trust you. Get with your man Rich and see what yall come up with and whatever yall come up with I'll give you on consignment fair enough? Hell Yeah! I ain't gone let you down Sanchez that's my word. Sanchez had a few of his men escort Kareem off the yacht and down to car. Sanchez right hand man Revi shook Kareem hand and told him to drive safe back to Savannah. Kareem hopped in the car and headed back home thinking to himself damn we about to be the man. When Kareem made it back home he a conversation with Rich. He convinced Rich to buy 20 kilos at $18,000 per kilo. In Savannah kilos was goin for $25,000 a piece with no problem. Aye Rich he also told me whatever we buy he'll give us on consignment. Damn Florida boy must be really got it made. Hell Yeah! Sanchez had a yacht docked at the port of Miami with some bad mix breed bitch with some phat asses. Man Rich one bitch kept walking pass my chair asking me papi you want another drink. I started to lean over and kiss the bitch on her ass cheek. Man Kareem you tripping. I could've seen Florida boy men tossing yo ass off the side of that yacht for doing some stupid shit like that. I'm just sayin Rich the bitch was bad (lol). Aye Kareem but on another note if we sold each kilo for $25,000 a piece and gave Florida boy back his $360,000 we would make a profit of $240,000. Rich that's major bread. Get with smitty and Dollar and let's make it happen. Rich, Kareem, Smitty and Dollar set out to take over the projects. The had a game plan. Instead of bo guarding their way in the game they figured if they set up a meeting with every major drug dealer in Fellwood homes and West Savannah and offered them a better price than the competition than everybody could make money and be happy. The hood loved Rich. Rich gave everybody a chance to make some real paper. Rich let all his customers know if they purchase cocaine from him he would cook it for them for a small fee. The whole city knew Rich was the best in the kitchen. I'm talking about stupid wrist game. Rich could stretch 28 grams of cocaine longer than a runway at the airport. Rich and his crew had the projects on lock flooding West Savannah with 100% pure cocaine. West Savannah was like a baby New York the city that never sleeps. The J's did anything for the high. Shoplifted, stole from family members and sold food stamps off their EBT cards. Some women even sold pussy, ass and bomb ass head for the high. Rich spot somewhat reminded you of the carter off New Jack City. It was like a one stop shop. You could've brought pussy, crack cocaine, and set inside the crack house and got high. For the passed 7 months Rich was pushing cocaine and spending more time with Kareem, Smitty and Dollar making money neglecting Alexis and she was really fed up with his bullshit. She decided to call her best friend Ronnie to ride with her over to the projects to check Rich. Ronnie is a ruthless bitch down for whatever with nothing to loose. When Alexis called her she was always down to ride. Alexis pulled into the projects and spotted Rich, Kareem and two females. One female was Kareem girlfriend keke and the other one was keke cousin Ronda. Alexis jumped out the car furious with Ronnie tailing her. Rich can tell from the look on her face that it's about to go down. Muthafucka you got 2 seconds to tell me who the fuck these bitches are? Why they here? And why I haven't been seeing you? Ronda jumped off the car yelling yo mama a bitch. Before Ronda could finish her sentence Ronnie was on her ass like flies on shit. Kareem yelled to Rich getcho hoes fam. Alexis turned around and rushed Kareem calling him a pussy nigga and screaming fuck you. The bitch you got on your side a hoe. Kareem shouted back fuck you too bitch. You coming around here stressin my nigga out Aye Rich the police coming up the street As the police officers got near Rich realized that it was his worst nightmare officer Giles and spike. All of the hustlers out of West Savannah gave officer Giles partner officer Grafton the nickname spike because he was always poking and fuckin with the young hustler. Officer Giles and Grafton have a long history with Rich. They sent Rich away for trafficking cocaine. But after 5 months Rich was released and back on the streets. Officer Giles and Grafton arrested Rich more than 10 times throughout their careers as a police officer. But thanks to the team of lawyers Rich had on retainer he was always able to beat the charges. Sargent Giles and officer Grafton promised themselves that before they retire they were going to put Rich away for a very long time. Alexis looked back at Ronnie and said let's go girl. I can't believe this muthafucka let his homeboy disrespect me. As Alexis and Ronnie approached the car tears started running down her face. Her voice Trimble as she spoke. Ronnie i love Rich. Why is he mistreating me? I don't know friend but just know i love you and I got your back. I love you too girl thanks for having my back. Ronnie I promise you Rich and Kareem gone pay big time. Alexis and Ronnie jumped back in there car speeding off driving like a bat outta hell. When they exited the projects they turned on the ramp that leads back to the HWY. They merged into traffic and noticed they were being followed by the police officers who bypassed them in the projects. The police officers hit the lights and pulled Alexis and Ronnie over. Both officers stepped out the car and approached Alexis car. When they got near the car they tap on the window. Alexis rolled the window down slow and asked is there a problem officers. Yes ma'am can you step out and come to the rear of the car. What's the problem officer. Do you know Richard Wright? Yes "he's my fiancé." Ok "Was he bothering you? Let me know because I'll take out a warrant out on his black ass for simple battery. No" We good. You sure? Yes I'm sure. Sargent Giles hated the ground Rich walked on. Spike added his two cents. You need to leave his ass alone. Rich is a bad person him and his wannabe thug friend. I hate them all. As spike spoke his face got redder by the second. The thought of Rich ballin riding around in cars that would take him a life time to get made him wanna kill Rich on sight Sargent Giles spoke again. Rich is putting drug on my streets and I can't have that. Officer Giles and Grafton told Alexis rich must be locked up and put away by any means. Take my card and call me if you ever need me. Alexis got back in the car and Ronnie asked so what did they want. Girl they is out to get Richard. Those two officers really hate Rich. They said Rich is putting poison on their streets and they can't have that and Rich had to be locked up and thrown away.

Later on that day, Alexis called Rich. Rich answered the phone on the fourth ring. "Wazzup, baby?"

"Look, Richard, we really need to talk. Those cops from the projects pulled me over. They know what kind of cars you, Smitty, Kareem, and Dollar drive and where y'all hang out at in Fellwood."

"Really? They know all that?"

"Yes, baby, they really do."

"You didn't give them any information, did you?"

"No, baby, I would never do that. Rich, are you coming home tonight, baby? I really miss you."

"Yeah, I'm coming home tonight, baby. I'll be in about 10:00 p.m."

"Okay, I love you, Rich."

"I love you more, Alexis. Muah!"

That night, Rich kept his word and went home to spend some much-needed time with his fiancée. When Rich got home, he noticed Alexis had prepared a nice hot meal. The two discussed their relationship problem over a glass of wine.

The next day in the projects, Rich, Kareem, and Dollar saw everybody running for their life. They all looked at one another, like what the hell is goin' on? Rich saw two teenagers, a young lady, and three crackheads running full speed, yelling, "Rico comin'! Rico comin'!" Rico was a powder head and stickup kid. He would go around the neighborhood terrorizing the drug dealers and extorting them. He was like the real 50 Cent from Queens, New York. The stickup kid. You'd rather had the devil on your ass than to have Rico on your ass. You either paid him an extortion fee or got robbed. Rico robbed Dollar two years ago. Dollar thought to himself, *This would be the perfect time to finally kill this fuckboy.*

When Rico came through the projects cut, he saw Rich and Kareem pointing at the crackheads who few by. They were so focused on the crackheads they never saw Rico easing up on them, holding a shotgun inside his trench coat.

"Kareem and Rich, just the niggas I been lookin for." Rico turned the corner fifteen seconds too late; he never saw Dollar slip off. Dollar went to the trunk of his car and grabbed his AR-15. Dollar eased back around the opposite side where Rico had Rich and Kareem cornered in.

"Wazzup, chumps? What y'all lame ass niggas for me? Run them pockets."

"Man, we don't have shit for you."

Just as Rico was about to pull out his shotgun, he felt the cold steel pressed up against the back of his head. Rico turned around, shocked to see Dollar standing in front of him, holding an automatic weapon in his face.

"What ya gon' do with that assault rifle, bitch-ass nigga besides make me mad?" Rico flinched at Dollar. *Boom!* Dollar pushed Rico back, leaving his lifeless body in the middle of the projects. Nobody ever really gave a damn about Rico. Rico was death struck; he had it coming. People around the neighborhood were just surprised it didn't happen earlier.

Dollar looked at Rich and Kareem and asked, "What are y'all about to do? It's about to be hot as a bitch around here."

"Yeah, I know. Police are about to be around here heavy. Let's shut the spot down for a couple of days just to see how things go."

"Aye, Kareem, what ya about to do?"

"I'm about to go pick up Keke and hit the sports bar and have a few drinks."

"Man, Kareem, ask Keke where her fine-ass cousin Ronda at when you get around here."

"Fo sho, Rich. I got ya, my nigga."

Just as Rich was about to head into the house for tonight to spend some time with Alexis, his phone started ringing. The song "Sex Me" by R. Kelly was playing through the phone speakers, so he knew who it was. He only had that ringtone set for one person—sexy-azz Ronda.

"Wazzup, sexy?"

"Nothing much. Home, bored, is ever lying in the bed watching *Paid in Full*. You wanna come over and keep me company?"

"Of course. I would love to come keep you company."

*****

"So I see you like gangsta movies, huh?"

"I love *Paid in Full*. That's my favorite movie, Rich."

"I bet it is."

"So, Mr. Rich kid, what are you doing?"

"I'm just chillin', hittin' a few corners."

"I think you should go to Daiquiri Island and grab me and you a drink and slide through."

"Okay, cool. Sounds like a plan."

CHAPTER 7

The alarm on Sevyn's car started going off, interrupting Rich and Sevyn. Sevyn jumped up and ran to the back door with Rich following close behind him. When he opened the back door, he saw kids playing kickball in the street. He saw the kid from the other day who ran up to him and asked for a dollar as he bent down, lookin' at his face in the rim on the luxury vehicle.

"Hey, li'l man." The li'l fella turned around and jumped up and then ran over to Sevyn. "What ya name, li'l man?"

"My name Carter."

"Carter, what ya doin'?"

"I'm lookin' at dis fresh car. Me and my friends saw dis car comin' up the street, and I called bingo first, so dat mean dis my car."

Rich and Sevyn couldn't help but laugh. "You like that car, li'l Carter?"

"Yeah, dis jive fresh."

"I tell you what, li'l Carter, stay in school and get you a good education. You'll be able to afford this car when you get older." Sevyn took his hand into his back pocket and pulled out a stack of money and gave li'l Carter a $20 bill.

"Thank you."

"You welcome. Go buy you and your friends something from the store."

Li'l Carter put the $20 bill in his pocket and then took off running through the project cut, leaving his friends to finish playing kickball and totally ignoring everything Sevyn just told him.

Rich said, "Shid li'l Carter said fuck that shit. He keeping the whole $20 for his self."

They burst out laughing as they headed back into the house.

*****

"Damn, Rich, that Rico kat was really about that life, huh?"

"Hell no. Rico was a pussy who preyed on the weak."

"Yo, Rich, Imma get up outta here. I gotta hot date."

"Go 'head, young nigga. Do yo thang and be careful and don't let that li'l honey be your downfall."

Sevyn thought to himself, *What the hell is Rich talking about?* When he got in the car, he let the sunroof back and put in his 8Ball & MJG Cd. When he pulled off, the music started blasting through the speakers. Just like candy. Sevyn was feelin' like the man as he rode through the projects. When he hit the corner, he saw li'l Carter and his friends jumpin' up and down, pointing at his car. The sun was catchin' that candy on his S550 Benz. He hit the east side, turning off Anderson Street on to Waters Avenue. Every bitch standing on the corner screamed Sevyn's name, wanting to jump in his car. After all that talkin' with Rich, Sevyn was hungry. So he hit up his favorite spot, Linda's Seafood.

When he got there, he ordered one pound of fried shrimps, two devil crabs, and one lobster tail and then walked across the street to the liquor store and ordered a fifth of gray goose and a Minute Maid cranberry juice. After he got his liquor, he walked back over to Linda's Seafood to pick up his food. Sevyn decided to take it in for tonight after his long visit to the projects.

The next day, Sevyn woke up around two in the afternoon. It was a nice hot sunny day, so Sevyn decided to pull out his 760 BMW Li and drove a few blocks. Sevyn's BMW was cocaine white with the buck interior. He always compared his car to Janet Jackson, saying, "Damn, this bitch looks good." He hit Tara up, and she answered in a low tone, as if she was sleep.

"Hey, mister, what have you been up to all day?"

"Nothing, really. I just came. I was riding through Fellwood Homes Projects to go holla at my people for a second."

"Baby, I hate that project."

"Why? It's not that bad."

"I had some bad memories in that project, and my ex-boyfriend is from there as well."

"What ya doin' tonight?"

"Nothing! Let's hit the club tonight. Club ICE is goin down tonight."

"Okay. I'll be ready about twelve o'clock."

Tara stopped going to the club years ago, but she liked Sevyn, so she couldn't tell him no. When they arrived at the club, Sevyn valeted his car in the VIP section and entered the club. It was packed from wall to wall. The bouncer showed them their section. Sevyn stopped the waitress and ordered two bottles of champagne. Sevyn noticed everybody watching and pointing at Tara. Sevyn said to himself, "Yeah, that's right, haters. Look all you want, but she with me. I got the baddest bitch in the club." Sevyn loved that fact that Tara was ten years older than him. It made him feel like he was the man.

Sevyn felt the champagne getting the best of him. After a long night of partying, Sevyn told Tara, "Baby, it's time to go." They walked out of the club to VIP section so Sevyn could pick up his car form valet parking. While they waited for the car to pull, Sevyn was hugging and kissing Tara.

"Baby, I hope you ready for our sweet lovemaking session that's about to go down when we make it back to your place."

"Baby, not tonight."

"Why?"

"Because it's that time of the month. My cycle is on, and besides, I gotta be somewhere at 10:00 a.m."

"Okay."

They listened to Anthony Hamilton as they cruised through the streets of East Savannah. Sevyn dropped Tara off home before he took it in for tonight. He flipped his cell phone open and called Tracy. "Hello! Tracy, I made it in safe."

"Fuck off, Sevyn."

"Damn, Tracy."

"Ain't no damn, Tracy. Why did you leave me? You know I wanted to go to the projects with you."

"My bad."

"Well, we will go tomorrow."

"Okay. I'm about to get some rest."

"Me too. I'll get with you tomorrow afternoon."

"Good night, bestie."

"Good night, lame."

The next day, Sevyn went to scoop Tracy up. She noticed he was driving his BMW.

"So you must've gone out last night."

"Yeah, me and Tara hit up club ICE."

"Oh, really!"

"Yeah, really."

"Must be nice. That girl got you wide open. Ever since you hooked up with her, you have been smelling yourself. You doing things with her you ain't never did with me, and I been seeing less of you."

"Tracy, you sound like you my girlfriend."

"No, I don't."

"Aww, somebody's jealous. Tracy, you not my girlfriend, and I'm not fucking you."

"So you did fuck that bitch? You know what, Sevyn, don't say shit to me. I'm pissed the fuck off."

When Sevyn and Tracy arrived in Fellwood, the projects was jam-packed. Rich was throwing a block party for the entire hood, free food and drinks for everybody. When they stepped out the Beamer, Sevyn spotted li'l Carter. He pointed at Sevyn's car and took off running full speed. He ran straight up to Sevyn's car. When he got up to the car, he placed his hands on the windows to get a better view. Than he stepped back and looked at the rims.

"Yo, wazzup, li'l Carter?"

"Bingo."

"Dis my car."

Li'l Carter screamed out, "Hey, mister, you know my name but ya ain't told me yo name."

My name's Sevyn."

"Mr. Sevyn, you gotta nudda fresh car?"

"Yeah. You remember what I told you right?"

"Yeah."

"What I said?"

"Stay in school and get a good education, and when I get older, I'll be able to afford one."

"You got it, li'l Carter. Imma holla at ya."

"Okay."

When Sevyn and Tracy was about to walk off, they saw li'l Carter staring at them with the biggest bug eyes ever.

"Come here, li'l Carter. Here is five dollars."

Li'l Carter took the money and said thank you and then took off running in the crowd. When Sevyn looked up, he saw Rich and his cousin Stutter Box waving from a distance. As they made their way through the crowd, they finally reached Rich and Stutter Box. Rich turned around and guided them between the projects cuts to where his black on black GL450 Benz truck was parked. Cars filled the parking lot as the young hustlers smoked on the best weed money can buy. When they made it to the parking lot, Tracy spotted Dollar three cars down talking to Smitty. Her juice box got wet as soon as she saw him. Just the thought of him alone drove her crazy. She wondered if his dick game was A1. Just as Rich, Sevyn, and Tracy were reaching for the door handles on the Benz truck, Dollar called Tracy's name.

"Yo, Tracy, wazzup, sexy?"

"Nothing much. Wazzup with you?"

"I'm just coolin', enjoyin' the cookout or block party or whatever you wanna call it. I'm sayin, Tracy, come kick it with me."

"Okay." Tracy let the door handle go and made her way over to where Dollar was at, leaving Rich and Sevyn to talk alone. Tracy walked up to Dollar and gave him a hug.

"Damn, Dollar, you smell good. What ya got on?"

"I got on David off cool water."

Tracy hopped in Dollar's Audi A7, which was two-tone light gray at the top and silver at the bottom with gray leather interior black carpet and wood grain everywhere. When they pulled off, Tracy fastened her seatbelt and sat back. The car was going so smooth it felt like they were riding on air.

"Hey, Tracy, you smoke?"

"No, not really, but I'll blow one with you."

"You drink?"

"Hell yeah! I get fucked up too."

"I got some gray goose and cranberry juice in the back. Pour us up a drink."

"Okay."

"I want light juice in my drink."

They hit the highway smoking and drinking, getting fucked up. After their smoke session, Dollar blurted out, "Man, Tracy, I'm so high."

Tracy immediately said, "Me too. Dollar, Imma keep it real with you."

'I don't mind if you do. Wazzup, baby girl?"

"That Grey Goose got my pussy throbbin'."

"So what ya sayin', baby girl?"

"I wanna fuck you. I wanna feel you inside of me."

"Baby girl, you sure this what you want?"

"I said it, ain't it?"

Dollar agreed and told Tracy to say less. Tracy wasn't going to fuck Dollar, but after finding out about Sevyn fucking Tara, she felt like no lines were being crossed. Dollar stopped by the convenient store to get some condoms and an energy drink and then headed to his spot. When he turned on his street, he saw a couple of detective cars across the street from his house to the young couple's house. But it was nothing new to him. The cop were always there do to the domestic violence between the young couple.

Tracy and Dollar rode around until the coast was clear. When they finally made it to Dollar's spot, he pulled in the garage, and they both got out. The two entered the house, and Tracy asked Dollar if she could use the bathroom.

"Yeah, sure. It's down the hall to your right." Dollar cut on his slow jams music and headed to the kitchen to roll up another blunt. When Tracy walked back up the hallway with her clothes in her hand, Dollar stopped rolling the blunt of Sour Diesel to admire her flawless body. Dollar's mouth dropped to the floor, seeing how beautiful Tracy's body was. Tracy dropped her clothes on the kitchen floor and then hopped on the kitchen countertop and spread her legs wide open, exposing her pretty pink juice box. She stuck one finger in her pussy, pulling it out slow and then placing it in her mouth and motioning for Dollar to come see what the game he'd been missing with the other finger. Still shocked at what he was seeing and what was about to take place, Tracy started talking.

"Look, Dollar, we don't have that long, so make it worth my while."

With no hesitation, Dollar got buck naked and approached the kitchen countertop. He leaned over and began eating her pussy while gripping her ass, driving Tracy's mind and soul wild and bringing her to three orgasms in just a short time. Tracy screamed, "I wanna feel you inside of me," so he let her down off the countertop, slid his condom on, and bent her over and started long dickin' her, causing her juices to build up around her ass crack and run down the side of her thighs, making her climax all over herself. When they finished they made their way to the bathroom to clean themselves up and head back to the block party.

*****

Rich and Sevyn sat in the truck chopping it up. "Yo, Rich, I like what ya doin' in the hood. That's mad love, big homie."

Rich smiled before he spoke. "Sevyn, I don't have a point to prove to nobody to show love. My people know I do this type of shit from the heart. That's why the hood love me."

"I respect that, Rich."

"It's all good, Sevyn, but back to business."

"Yeah, back to business."

CHAPTER 8

Rich pulled up to Daiquiri Island and parked in the front so he could run in and come right back out. When he got inside the Daiquiri spot, he ran into Buttahead.

"Yo, Rich kid, wazzup, baby?"

"I'm I goin to get that dick up out ya tonight or what?"

"Man, Buttahead, gone head now and stop playing."

"I ain't playing. I want that dick tonight for real."

"Okay, Imma call you later on tonight, 'bout twelve."

"Rich, don't bullshit me 'cause you know how you do. You said that same shit last time."

Rich burst out laughing, knowing she was tellin' the truth. "Man, Buttahead, I'm for real this time."

"Well, we gon' see."

She got the nickname Buttahead because everything on her body looked good but her head. Rich used to always tell Dollar, Kareem, and Smitty Buttahead was one of the ugliest red bones he'd ever seen.

Ten minutes later, Rich dashed out the door with two large cups of Long Island iced tea in his hand, leaving Buttahead standing there lookin' stupid. He jumped back in his whip and began swerving through traffic. It took twenty minutes to make it from Daiquiri Island to Ronda's house. Rich made it there in a record-breaking time, eight minutes flat. When he pulled up, Ronda was already standing on the front porch waiting on him. He walked up on the porch and planted a wet kiss on her cheek.

"Wazzup, sexy?"

"I'm horny, that's wazzup."

"Well, you called the right guy."

Rich and Ronda sipped on their Long Island iced teas until they were gone, and with no talkin', Ronda got up off the sofa and began to get naked. Rich's eyes was glued to her body as he admired God's work. She pulled him slowly down the hallway to her bedroom and started undressing him. Once Rich was naked, his erect penis was on full display. Ronda laid him back on the bed and began licking on his chest and stroking his large manhood. Rich guided her head down to his dick. And just like a veteran, she took the whole dick into her mouth, making it disappear. Rich felt like he was in heaven with his eyes rolling in the back of his head and his toes curled up so tight it damn near ripped holes in his socks. Ronda felt Rich's dick jumping and knew what that meant, so she stopped sucking and bent over, busting that pretty pink pussy open.

"Come on, daddy, and hit this pussy from the back."

Rich stood to his feet and entered her wetness. Ronda started throwing her voluptuous ass back harder and faster in every direction, knocking Rich off balance and causing him to stumble. Rich thought it was time to take control. He pinned Ronda's ass down and began driving his dick in and out her pussy like a madman, causing her to damn near have an orgasm. Minutes later, her legs tightened up, so he knew she was about to climax. He flipped her over and started eating her pussy like it was the Last Supper. Rich drove Ronda crazy as he sucked on her clitoris, rotating his tongue in circular motion. Ronda started moaning louder and louder. This turned Rich on, so he began to talk to her.

"Whose pussy is this?"

Ronda tensed up and looked back and said, "This yo pussy, daddy."

Rich was literally trying to eat Ronda's pussy so good until her soul left her body. Ronda looked Rich dead in his eyes and asked, "Baby, what are you doin' to me?"

Rich replied, "I'm tryna eat yo pussy so good until your heart stops."

Ronda arched her back up as her legs began to shake. "Baby, I'm about to climax." Just as Rich was about to get up, she exploded all over his face. When Rich stood to his feet, his face looked like a glazed doughnut.

The two lovebirds took a nice hot shower after fucking each other's brains out. When they returned to the bedroom, Rich got into bed and up under the covers, and Ronda joined him soon after laying her head on his chest while whispering in his ear, "Baby, I love you."

"I love you too."

"Rich, you not going to break my heart, are you?"

"No, baby, never will I do that."

"You promise?"

"Yes, baby, I promise."

Ronda fell asleep while Rich gazed at the ceiling, realizing that he just fucked up by making Ronda a promise that he knew he was going to eventually break.

The next morning, Rich woke up alone, realizing Ronda was gone. She left a note on the nightstand.

> Good morning, sexy face. I had to step out and go handle some business. I made you some breakfast, your favorite—eggs, bacon, and pancakes with strawberries on the side. When you eat the strawberries, I want you to think of me. LOL. Have a blessed day, and I want to see you tonight.
> Love you.

Rich ate breakfast, got dressed, and then went on his way. When he made his way through West Savannah, the hood looked like a ghost town—not one dope fiend insight. Rich turned on West Street where he saw Smitty posted up like a light pole. So Rich decided to pull over and holla at him.

"Yo, Smitty, wazzup, big-timer? You out early, ain't it?"

"Shid, Rich. You know, I gotta make that money." Smitty had this old-school saying, "The early bird gets the worm." Rich was familiar with the old-school saying. "Man, Rich, shit been kinda slow around here lately. You know, somebody knocked that nigga Rico top off."

"For real?"

"Hell yeah. Left that nigga's body stankin'. And the fucked-up part about it, Rich, they left the body in the middle of the projects on the ground for about ten hours before the funeral home people came and got him."

"Damn, Smitty, that's fucked up. But you know how it goes— when you livin' by the gun, you die by the gun."

"That's true, Rich."

"Say, Smitty, you saw Kareem or Dollar around here?"

"Yeah, earlier."

"Okay. Imma holla at ya, Smitty." Rich rolled up his window and eased off from the curb. He then picked up his phone and dialed Dollar's number, and the voice mail came straight on, so he decided to call Kareem.

Kareem answered the phone and asked, "Rich, wazzup, lover boy?"

"Shit just coolin'. I just came outside. Me and Dollar over here in Bayview Project chillin' at Bayview Jizzle's spot. We about to head to the basketball court. I'm 'bout to take these niggas to flight school."

Bayview Jizzle shouted through the phone, "Man, Rich, these can't fuck with me. Jmma show love out here on the court today, Rich. I'm 'bout to shoot Kareem and Dollar's eyes out."

"Aye, Kareem, I'm 'bout to ride over there. It's dead as hell in Fellwood."

"Okay, come through."

Fifteen minutes later, Rich pulled up in Bayview. Bayview was the other projects on the opposite side of Bay Street where the street hustler played basketball on Sunday. Rich parked his whip and got out and walked on the basketball.

"Yo, Dollar, let me get a shot 9 Swish all net nigga."

"Damn, Bayview Jizzle, I still got it, my nigga."

Dollar sucked his teeth. "Man, whatever. That was luck."

"Nigga, you crazy. Lucky, my ass. Aye, Dollar, I'm supposed to go play pro ball for the Knicks."

"Well, what happened, Mr. Rich kid?"

"Nigga, I chose the wrong game."

Kareem, Dollar, and Bayview Jizzle bust out laughing. Dollar asked, "Rich man, what ya gon' do, go to sleep and dream about the shit you gon' say the next day? And speaking of dreamin', where you stay at last night? And don't lie because we already know, nigga."

"Well, if you know, what ya ask for?"

"Just to see you gon' keep it real with us. We heard Ronda put that pussy on last night. Put you straight to sleep, had you in her bed stretched out like Jordan." Dollar was anxious to know what happened, so cuttin' straight to the chase, he asked, "Aye, Rich kid, you ate the pussy?"

"Hell yeah! Ate that pussy like it was the last meal for the week."

"Goddamn!"

Bayview Jizzle looked at Kareem and Dollar and said, "Rich, Ronda got ya fucked up and you only got the pussy one time."

Kareem dropped his head and then lifted it back up and said, "Man, Rich, Alexis gon' kill both of y'all ass, and I don't wanna be nowhere around."

"Kareem, I always say, what she don't know won't hurt her. And how y'all know I was over there?"

"Because she called Keke early this morning and told her. That's who came and pick her up from the house this morning."

Rich's phone started vibrating, so he stuck his hand in his pocket to retrieve it and R. Kelly's "Sex Me" ringtone was playing, so he knew who it was. "Ronda, wazzup, baby?"

"Nothin'. I was just callin' you to let you know your trap phone was on the nightstand."

"Okay, put it up for me, baby. I'm on my way to get it."

Rich pulled up to Ronda's house and got out. He walked on the side of the house and slid in through the back door. When he made it to Ronda's room, he grabbed his phone and noticed the water running in the bathroom, so he opened the door and stuck his head in and saw Ronda inside the shower.

*****

Alexis was 500 degrees. Rich lied again. She was riding around with Ronnie lookin' for Rich. She was sure to kill him this time. Ronnie spotted Rich's white Range Rover truck, so the two ladies pulled into the convenience store parking lot across the street from where Rich's truck was parked. They felt like police on a stakeout, trying to see which house Rich would come out of. Two hours had passed and the ladies grew tired and were about to leave when the front door came flying open, and out walked Rich. Seconds later, Ronda walked out on the porch.

"What the hell! Ronnie, Imma kill that bitch. That's the bitch from the projects." Alexis was so hurt that she was willing to do anything for revenge. She dropped Ronnie off and made a phone call and one last stop before she went in for the night.

Later that night, Alexis called Rich's phone, and his phone went straight to the voice mail. So she decided to call back. This time, he answered, "Hey, love."

"Don't give me that love bullshit. Richard, why must you lie and cheat on me? I don't deserve this. You just continue to hurt and mistreat me. First, you lied about coming home last night, and on top of that, I watched you come out of that bitch Ronda's house today. Are you fuckin' her? And don't lie because if I find out you are, Imma kill her. And yo ass is fish grease."

"No! I'm not fuckin' her."

CHAPTER 9

One day, three months later, Ronda got off from work late. She was so tired from working a double shift that she never even paid attention to the black Volkswagen sitting across the street from her house. When she placed her key in the door, she felt the steel of a 9mm pressed up against the back of her head and a .38 revolver to her back.

"Bitch, open the door and don't look back."

She did as she was told. When the door opened, the two intruders hit Honda with the butt of the gun in her head, causing her to pass out for thirty minutes. When Honda woke up, she was greeted by two masked men. When they removed their mask, Honda shit a brick when she saw the face of Alexis and Ronnie.

"Now Imma ask you a question and I want one answer. Are you fuckin' Rich?"

Ronda was so down for Rich that she was willing to risk her own life. She told Alexis to go to hell and jumped up and rushed her, knocking the gun out of her hand. The two went toe to toe. Ronda got the best of Alexis and grabbed her gun off the floor. But before she could get a shot off, Ronnie bust her in the arm, causing her to drop the gun. Alexis picked up the gun and walked up and stood over Ronda.

"You told me to go to hell. I am going, just not before you, bitch." *Boom!*

*****

Two days later, Keke called Rich. "Hello?"

"Hey, wazzup, Rich kid?"

"Wazzup, what's good, Keke?"

"Have you talked to Ronda?"

"No! I've been calling her for the past two days but I haven't gotten an answer. You know what, Keke, Imma go by her house and check on her right now. I'll call you in twenty minutes when I reach her crib." He hung up. "Aye, Smitty, ride with me over to Ronda's house."

Rich and Smitty arrived at Ronda's place in exactly twenty minutes. When they parked, Rich got out first, leaving Smitty in the car smoking on cigarette. He knocked, but no one answered. Rich yelled for Smitty. When Smitty hopped out the car, he out he his cigarettes and then approached Rich.

"Aye, Smitty, go check the side door."

"Okay."

One minute later, Smitty came back running to the front porch. "Aye, Rich."

"Yeah?"

"Man, hurry up. You gon' believe this shit."

When Rich and Smitty entered the house, the first thing they saw was Ronda's dead body. Smitty called the police now. He went in the front room and looked down and spotted a 9mm bullet casing and picked it up to go show Rich. "Rich, look what I found. It's a 9mm bullet casing."

"Man, Smitty, put that shit down." Rich called Keke, but her voice mail came straight on.

*****

Back on the other side of town at Keke's crib, she was blasting The Isley Brothers in between the sheets through the speakers, sipping on Chardonnay wine and cooking her favorite ghetto meal—pork and beans, white rice, and beef sausage. When the food was done, she cut it off and walked in her room just in time to catch the 6:00 p.m. news. Breaking news flashed across the TV, catching Keke's attention. It was about a fatal shooting on the east side of Savannah, leaving one woman dead. Twenty-two-year-old Ronda Sanders was found dead from two gunshot wounds—one in head and another one in the arm. Keke dropped her wineglass on the floor and fell to her knees, screaming and crying, asking God why.

*****

"Hey, Kareem, man, you not goin' to believe this shit. Me and Smitty found Ronda dead."

"Hold up, Rich, slow down. You talkin' too fast."

"Well, nigga, Imma say it slow as possible. Me and Smitty found Ronda dead. Did you hear me that time? Call Keke and let her know."

"Okay, I'm about to." Kareem called Keke. "Yo, Keke, I hate to bring you this bad news, but Ronda is dead. Somebody shot her."

Still not believing what she just saw on the news, she gathered her thoughts together and said, "Kareem, baby, tell me I'm dreaming."

"I wish I could, honey. Keke, you and the rest of your family really need to get over here."

*****

Rich, Smitty, Kareem, Dollar, and Keke sat in the front row of the funeral and paid their respect. After the funeral, they sat there, thinking who could have done this and why. Rich told Kareem, "It's getting too crazy around here. Imma just lie low, Kareem. Aye, Kareem."

"Wazzup, Rich kid, talk to me."

"This is it. I got one more run in me and I'm out the game for good. Set up the meeting with Florida boy. Tell him we want sixty bricks.

Kareem gave Smitty the last two bricks to take back to the hood for the li'l homies before he took off to Miami. On the way to West Savannah, Smitty made a quick stop by his house to take a shower.

When he was in the shower, his girlfriend, Sha'meka, came and knocked on the bathroom door.

"Yeah, wazzup, baby?"

"Imma make a quick store run. I'll be right back."

"Okay, love."

When Sha'meka jumped in the car and backed out the driveway, Sergeant Giles and Officer Gratton was parked on the corner doing paperwork when they spotted Smitty's car. They thought, *This would be a perfect time to infiltrate Rich's clique.* Sergeant Giles hit the lights, pulling Sha'meka over just a few blocks away from her house. When they searched the car, they found two kilos and placed Sha'meka under arrest for drug trafficking. She was taken to Chatham County detention center and processed. She called Smitty, upset and crying.

"Baby, I'm in jail."

"Sha'meka, for what?"

"That Officer Spic or Spike, whatever his name is, and Officer Giles pulled me over and found drugs in your car. My bail hearing is in the morning."

"Sha'meka's bail was set at $10,000, but Smitty only had $5,000, so he decided to hit up Rich to borrow the other $5,000. Word traveled throughout the city so fast about Sha'meka getting busted with two bricks. So for Rich to get a call from Smitty just seemed outta pocket. When Smitty called Rich the first time, it went to the voice mail on the first ring and the second time on the third ring. Rich declined the call, and Smitty knew it and began to get mad, so he decided to call Alexis. When Alexis answered the phone, Smitty started crying.

"Lex, they got Meka."

"Who got Meka?"

Sergeant Giles and Spike dirty ass. Her bail is $10,000, but I only got $5,000. I called Rich to borrow the other $5,000, but he's not answering my calls. I honestly think Rich is sending me to the voice mail on purpose. I gotta get my girl out, Lex. Please help me."

Just then, a lightbulb went off in Alexis's head. Alexis thought how she could use Smitty to help her get revenge against Rich and

Kareem. "Okay, Smitty, I'll help you get your girl out that shithole, but you gotta help me."

"Anything you need, Lex."

"Anything?"

"Yes, anything."

"Okay."

"Thanks a lot, Lex."

"You welcome, Smitty." Alexis made a few phone calls, and just like that, after ten days of lockup time, Sha'meka was released.

CHAPTER 10

Kareem met with Sanchez as planned. Kareem trafficked cocaine from Miami up 1-95 to Savannah. When he got near Savannah, Kareem called Smitty and Dollar to help him unload the shipment of cocaine at the new stash spot. When Kareem arrived at the stash house, Dollar and Smitty were already in place.

The next day, Rich kid called a meeting to let the fellas know that this is his last run and he was getting out of the game for good. Smitty, Kareem, and Dollar was on their way to meeting. Rich called Kareem's phone. When he answered, Rich asked him to stop by his crib and grab his computer because he was too far out to turn around. Kareem told Rich, "I got ya, homie," and ended the call. Kareem made a detour and headed back to Rich's place. The other guys were on their way to the meeting as scheduled.

Smitty was the first to arrive at the stash house where the meeting was about to take place. When he entered the stash house, it was dark. So he went to cut the lights on but was snatched in the room by two gunmen. Scared and shaking like a bitch, Smitty was clearly caught off guard.

"Where the fuck is Kareem and Rich?"

"They're on the way."

"You better hope so because your bitch life is on the line."

"Twenty years to life is a long time."

"Look, Alexis, we had a deal. If I get ya Rich and Kareem, you, Spike, and Sergeant Giles would leave my girlfriend alone."

"Fuck that deal."

"Alexis, why are you doin' this?"

"Shut the fuck up. Yo sounding like a bitch."

"Payback is a bitch. Now get the fuck out and you better hope they show up, or else."

Ten minutes later, Dollar arrived and saw Smitty sweating bullets. "Yo, Smitty, you good, fam?"

"Yeah, I'm straight."

When Kareem reached Rich's house, he entered through the side door. He looked around the house for a second before he spotted the computer on the kitchen counter. Kareem wanted to check his e-mail before he dipped back out the door. When he flipped open the computer, he realized he grabbed Alexis's computer and not Rich's. So he powered it on, and what he saw made his heart stop. An e-mail sent to Sergeant Giles the previous day.

> Officer Giles, I have the information you asked for. Rich is buying sixty kilos, and Kareem is goin' to pick them up from Miami and traffic them back to Savannah and bring them to the stash house. Remember, this is the last run, so it's now or never.

Kareem was clueless as to how she found out about the meeting, but he damn sure in hell was going to get to the bottom of it. *What the fuck, this bitch Alexis is a snitch. I gotta get the fuck outta here. I have to warn my boy Rich kid before it's too late.* Kareem called Rich's phone, and the answering machine picked straight up. So he decided to call again and got the voice mail. After the eighth time and still no answer, he headed back out the side door. Kareem thought, *I gotta make it to the stash house ASAP and let the fellas know what's goin' on.* When Kareem got in his car and began to pull off, he was boxed in by the FBI and SPD and was placed under arrest.

Back at the stash house, Smitty was sitting in the car. Soon as Dollar walked in the stash house, he was swarmed by the FBI and DEA and taken into custody. Sergeant Giles and the FBI thought, *Sixty kilos of pure cocaine, these mothafuckas ain't never coming home.* Just before Rich arrived at the stash house, Smitty called him.

"Look, Rich, don't show up to the stash house. It's a setup."

"What the fuck you mean it's a setup?"

"Spike and his partners are waiting on you to arrive."

"Say it ain't so, Smitty. Tell me you ain't did what I think you did."

"I had to, Rich. SPD got Sha'meka for trafficking cocaine."

"You bitch ass nigga. I let you eat off my plate, and this is how you repay me. I knew there was a reason I ain't trusted you." Click.

After Dollar was taken into custody and Smitty made the phone call to Rich, he jumped in his car and sped away. Four blocks up the street, he was pulled over by local law enforcement. After they searched his car, they found a loaded pistol up under his seat. The detective jumped on the phone and made a phone call.

"Hey, boss, I think this is it. We got it. Imma go run ballistics tests now."

Smitty was taken into custody and down to Savannah head-quarters precinct downtown on Habersham Street. One hour later, Detective Martin walked into the interrogation, holding up a ziplock bag with a firearm in it and shell casings.

"Mr. Miller, where were you two weeks ago, May fifth at 4:18 p.m.?"

"I was home."

"You sure?"

"Yeah, I'm sure. Now I wanna go home."

"Mr. Miller, so you telling me May fifth three weeks ago at 3:18 p.m. you was home."

"Yeah, I was home."

"I see, Mr. Miller. You know you done fucked up, right?"

"But—"

"But my ass. You know you done fucked up, right, son?

"I'm not talking. Where is my lawyer?"

"Okay, tough guy. We found this loaded pistol in your car."

"That's not my shit."

"Your fingerprints were on the bullet casing found at the crime scene that was fired from this pistol. Mr. Miller, you are being charged with the murder of Ronda Sanders."

"Wait! That's not right. I wasn't there."

"Too late to talk now. Save it for the DA, the judge, and your lawyer."

*****

Rich had just a little over $400,000 in his safe back home. He figured he could catch Kareem at the house to inform him of the sucka shit Smitty had done and grab his money before he went on the run.

Rich called the only person he could count on—Alexis. Alexis answered and told Rich to hold on. When she returned to the phone, she asked him, "Wazzup?"

"Sweetie, I need you to meet me on the island to get me a room. The FBI and SPD is on my ass. Come alone and don't bring anyone with you."

Alexis beat Rich to the island to set her plan into motion. She decided to get a room at the Comfort Inn Suite. She had to make a run, so she texted Rich: *Baby, I have to make a run. I left the key at the front desk.* When Rich made it to the hotel, it was packed with out-of-town guests. So he slid in through the back door. He got the room key from the front desk and headed up to his room. When he entered the room, he turned the TV on and flopped across the bed. He saw a note with an ink pen next to it and decided to read.

Dear Richard,

I told you not to fuck over my love and heart. You cheated on me time after time. You even allowed your friends to disrespect me and you did nothing about it. I told you I was going to make your life a living hell. That's just what I planned on doin'. I told Kareem and the probation officer about y'all meeting and had them follow him. Now who's the hoe? I wasn't happy with you and I'll be damned if another bitch was gon' be happy with you. Yo bitch Ronda, I killed that bitch. See? Nothing beat the cross but the double cross bitch.

Rich couldn't believe what he just read. *This shit got to be a game*, he thought. Rich got up to go look out the window. The hotel was surrounded. *What the fuck! That dirty bitch set me up.* Rich decided to make a break for the door. Soon as he reached for the knob, the room door came flying open, and in came Sergeant Giles and the DEA.

"Freeze, you black son of a bitch. If you move an inch, Imma put so many bullet holes in your ass yo mama ain't gon' be able to identify yo black ass." Rich hated Sergeant Giles with a passion, and he knew it. "Cuff this piece of shit. You just don't know I waited years to put you away for a very long time."

Forty-two minutes later, they arrived at the headquarters to interrogate Rich. In walked two federal agents.

"Hi, Mr. Wright. My name is Agent Smith, and this is my partner, Agent Jackson. It's not you that we want. Give us your connection, Sanchez Lopez, and we will cut you a deal."

"I don't know a Sanchez Lopez. You got me fucked up, I know the game. I play this shit from A to Z, so you two mothafuckas can stick y'all heads up each other's ass. Take me to the county jail to meet my lawyer."

When Rich got to the jailhouse, he was booked and processed and then placed in 9-D where they housed all of other federal inmates. The first couple of days, Rich really just slept and wondered to himself how in the hell he let this happened. When he finally came out of the room, everybody was watching and pointing at him. Seeing that he and his crew made the new headline, Rich was well respected throughout the jailhouse. Every convict wanted to have a sit-down with him to see if they could get down with him and his crew.

Rich's roommate was this old Muslim kat with a lot of wisdom. He always told Rich, "Watch what ya say around these guys because most of them can't handle the time and looking for a way out. You hear me, young blood? I been watching you ever since you came in. I like the way you move. Most of these young dudes around here puttin' on a show, walkin' around with their chest pokin' out, braggin' about shit they used to do and shit they used to have. Let me tell you somethin', young blood. The streets judge you off what ya got now, what ya had back then, and the loudest one in the room is always the weakest one in the room. Remember that, young blood."

He continued, "So, young blood, what ya in this shithole for?"

"Drug conspiracy to commit a felony and possession of cocaine with the intent to distribute. What about you?"

"Murder!"

"Damn, Ahk, murder?"

"Hell yeah, murder. I killed this young stickup kid named La'Kid. He robbed me, and I had to murk his ass. See, young blood, he took a few hundreds. Next time, it just might've been my life."

Over the course of the next few months, Rich and Ahk just sat around playin' chess all day. Ahk schooled Rich to the game of life and how it's played. See, Ahk had a life sentence, so he planned on keeping a close eye on Rich once he was released. Rich would be his eyes and ears on the outside.

"Ahk, I have a court date coming up. How much time you think I'm lookin' at?"

"That I can't tell you a real answer, but whatever it is, you'll be able to handle it. Trust me."

CHAPTER 11

Six months later, Rich's trial was coming to an end. This was the day Sergeant Giles and Officer Gratton had been waiting for—the sentencing day. The judge asked that Rich stand beside his lawyer.

"Mr. Wright, you are charged with conspiracy to commit a felony and possession of cocaine with the intent to distribute. Do you wish to say anything before I sentence you?"

"Yes, I'd like to apologize to my kids and my family for the entire heartache I caused them. That's it."

"Okay. Mr. Wright, I hereby sentence you to 120 months. This court is adjourned."

The officers finally got what they wanted. They smirked at Rich and then exited the courtroom. When Rich returned from court, he went to find Ahk and inform him of the news.

"So how things turned out for you, young blood? They gave me 120 months, Ahk. Ten years."

"Not bad, young blood, considering you was facing three hundred months in the beginning. So what ya plan on doin' once you are released and back on the streets, young blood?"

"I'm planning on getting my life back on the right track with my two daughters and my auntie and go into the book publishing business."

"Sounds like a plan, young blood. I ain't got nothing but love fo ya. You got my support 100 percent."

"And I ain't got nothing but love for you too, Ahk."

The two turned their heads and focused on the TV when they saw breaking news flash across the screen. A fatal car accident left one officer dead. Officer Gratton was pronounced dead on the scene of the accident. Rich looked at Ahk and smiled and said, "God don't like ugly."

*****

Officer David Giles retired just like he said he would. He has a new lady in his life. David changed his nasty ways and catered to the leading lady in his life. He proposed to his fiancée and got married. While on honeymoon, he decided to spice things up in their relationship. She came out the bathroom with a silk robe on and some handcuffs in her hand. When she handcuffed his legs and arms to the bed, she opened her robe, exposing her nude body and tattoo. The tattoo read "Rich kid." David looked at his wife strange.

"Baby, who is Rich kid?"

"David, Rich kid is my nephew."

"Richard Wright?"

"Yes, the one you helped put away."

David's face turned firecracker red. Donna pulled out a 9mm. David begged for his life.

"Baby, please don't do it. I love you."

"I love you, too, but I love my nephew more." *Boom!*

David's lifeless body lay there handcuffed to the bed with his eyes still open as Donna exited the room.

"I hate pigs," she said.

CHAPTER 12

A young lady knocked on Rich's window.

"Here's your food, Rich kid."

"Thanks, Latasha."

"You welcome."

Sevyn sat up in his seat. "So, Rich, let me get this straight. So your girlfriend—well, ex-girlfriend—and Smitty set you up?"

"Correct."

"She had to be a cold mothafucka to kill a bitch and then turn around and set you and yo partnas up, real talk."

"Listen, Sevyn, I loved that girl, even considered marrying her. Sevyn, I never seen this shit coming. Now don't get me wrong, I don't like the fucked-up shit she done, but I understand why she did it. See, Sevyn, if Imma be real with you, then I gotta be real with myself first. Even though I loved her and was in love with her, I cheated on her time after time. I turned her into something she wasn't."

"And what was that, Rich?"

"A scorn woman, a killer, and a snitch."

"Damn, Rich, that's deep."

"It is, but it's also real. See, Sevyn, when I see you, I see myself. You remind me so much of myself. That's why I told you, don't let that new HI honey be your downfall."

Sevyn sat there thinking, *Damn, now it's starting to make sense.* "Rich, love is strong, powerful, and dangerous."

"I know, young blood, because it was a gift and a curse to me loving Tara."

"Tara! I thought you said her name was Alexis."

"It is, but when I'm in my feelings, I call her by her real name Tara. Tara is her first name."

"So what's her last name?"

"Jones."

"Get the fuck out of here, Rich. Man, Rich, you for real?"

"For real."

"Aye, Rich, gotta go."

"Where you goin' young blood? There's still so much more we have to talk about."

"I have to go handle some business."

"Okay. Be careful, young nigga, and remember what I told you. It only takes a split second to slip."

Sevyn slapped hands with Rich and hopped out the truck. He then called Tracy's phone.

"Hello?"

"Yo, Tracy, where are you?"

"Sittin' in the car with Dollar."

"Tracy, we have to leave ASAP. You not goin' to believe the shit I'm 'bout to tell you."

"Okay. I'm comin'."

Tracy got out of the car and headed for Sevyn's car. When she reached the car, she saw Sevyn leaning on the hood of his car with the most dumbfounded look on his face. "Friend, what's wrong?"

"Tracy, I fucked up big-time. Let's head back to the east side."

They both hopped in the car and pulled off.

"So, wazzup, Fresh? Talk to me."

"It's about Tara."

"What about that bitch?"

"Tara is Rich's ex-girlfriend. She's the one who set him, Kareem, and Dollar up, along with two dirty cops, David Giles and Adam Gratton, aka Spike."

"Oh, heard many stories about them two dirty cops. But I thought Rich's ex-girlfriend's name was Alexis."

"It is, but Tara is her real name. She goes by Tara to cover up all the dirty shit she done. The whole city knows about this dirty-ass bitch, but nobody knows her by Tara. Tracy, how could I be so blind and stupid to the fact?"

"Want me to keep it real with you?"

"Yes."

"Chasing a cute face and fat azz."

As much as Sevyn hated to admit it, she was right.

"I'm all in the club with this snitch-ass bitch. I'm thinking everybody lookin' at and pointin' at me because I got the baddest bitch in the club. They lookin' and pointin' because this bitch a snitch. Now I see why she hates Fellwood Homes Projects."

Tracy said, "Sevyn, I guess the joke was on you."

"I guess it was, Tracy."

"I told you I had a fucked-up feelin' about her. She wasn't right. Hey, Sevyn, what ya doin' tonight?"

"Nothin'. I'm too blown to party. I think Imma go in the house early tonight, kick back, and have me a drink."

"Oooh, can I come?"

"Yeah, why not."

When they got to Sevyn's crib, he told Tracy to make herself at home and then disappeared to his room to grab his polo pajamas to shower. Tracy came in his room and asked Sevyn if she could have a T-shirt to sleep in. She walked in and repeated herself.

"Sevyn, can I have a T-shirt?"

When Sevyn didn't respond, Tracy walked in his bathroom. Sevyn was standing up in the shower, letting the hot water soothe his body. He never noticed Tracy was gazing at his erect penis. He finally lifted his head up to see Tracy standing there. Sevyn tried to close the shower curtain but was too late.

"Tracy, how long have you been standing there?"

"Long enough to see that dick get bigger and bigger."

"All right, Tracy, this ain't what ya want."

"As a matter of fact, that is what I want."

Tracy got naked and hopped in the shower with Sevyn. She stroked his manhood as her pussy got wet. Tracy looked Sevyn dead in the eyes and told him to put it in. Sevyn did as he was told. He bent Tracy over and slid his dick into her wetness, causing her to jump and moan at the same time.

"Oooh, shit, Sevyn, this dick feels so good. Fuck me, baby. Give me every inch of that dick." The more she moaned and talked shit, the closer Sevyn came to busting a nut. After forty minutes of straight pounding and beating that pussy up, Tracy finally yelled, "I'm comin', baby, I'm comin'." When she climaxed, she turned and said, "Damn, Sevyn, that dick was on the one."

They finished up washing and got out of the shower. Sevyn went to his bed to put on his polo pajamas. Then he turned and reach in the dresser and grabbed Tracy a T-shirt. Sevyn exited the room and then headed to the kitchen to fix two drinks. They kicked it all night until they grew tired and went to bed.

The next morning, Tracy felt strange knowing that she fucked Dollar and Sevyn in the same day. Tracy went to Sevyn's room and woke him up and asked him to take her home. When they got in the car, Sevyn began to speak.

"Tracy, I feel like the biggest fool ever."

Don't feel that way. Just do better. Sevyn, I will never tell you anything wrong."

Before Tracy got out of the car, she leaned over and gave Sevyn the most passionate kiss ever and then backed up. She finally did something she always wanted to do, and that was kiss Sevyn's sweet lips.

"Sevyn?"

"Yeah, wazzup?"

"I love you."

"I love you more, Tracy."

Tracy stepped out of the car, and Sevyn grabbed her by the arm. "Hey, Tracy."

"Yes, Sevyn?"

"Thank you."

*****

Two months later, Sevyn was talking to Rebecca at the hair salon about some business that took place some time ago. Rebecca said, "Sevyn, I just—"

Before she could finish saying what she was about to say, Sevyn told her to hold up. "Tracy's callin' me. Yo, Tracy, wazzup?"

"Nothin' much. You gotta second?"

"Yeah, wazzup?"

"Sevyn, I need to tell you something."

"Okay, talk to me."

"I'm pregnant."

"Wait what! You pregnant?"

Rebecca said, "Yes, Sevyn, I'm pregnant."

The Downfall of a Hustler Part 2
Coming Soon

How in the hell is Sevyn going to explain to two females that work in the same hair salon he got both of them pregnant?

Rich is no stranger to the game and betrayal that comes with it. Rich and his crew have run Fellwood Homes Projects for a long time while trying to balance his relationship with his fiancée, Alexis. But when Alexis feels she's not getting the attention she needs and things start to go wrong, Alexis is forced to take action. At the same time, Rich is forced to fight back and stay clear of two dirty cops, Sergeant Giles and Officer Gratton, aka Spike, who is trying to tear him and his crew down. In the end, will Rich and his crew be able to stand tall in the streets they help build, or will they fall at the hands of the law?

G-Money is an author born in Savannah, Georgia. G-Money found a passion for writing urban fiction novels while incarcerated, facing federal drug conspiracy charges in hopes of one day becoming a *New York Times* bestselling author.